# SABOTAGE

Leaning back in an easy chair in the privacy of his cabin, Geiger watched his laptop screen intently with a slow smile spreading across his face.

The digital countdown was ending: 0:02. . . 0:01. . .

He closed his eyes and waited.

Meanwhile, in the engine room, the needles on all the engine dials moved into the red zone. The chief engineer was thinking it was a good thing all fire doors leading to the danger area had been sealed. Then he was lifted a foot off his chair by the shock of a nearby blast.

The exploding engine caused the ship to heel to one side. One end of the ballroom lifted up until the entire room was at an angle. Chairs, tables, anything not bolted to the floor slid from the high side of the ballroom to the low one. So did many of the passengers, dressed in their finery.

Chandeliers fell from the ceiling, and the crystals scattered beneath people's feet. Most passengers had given up all pretense at calm—they ran for their lives to the exit doors, pushing and shoving those who got in their way.

For Annie and Alex, who had been dancing locked in an embrace, the romantic mood of the evening was long gone. "Please, this is my vacation," she said to him. "I just want to relax . . . at least once."

Alex pointed to himself innocently. "I had nothing to do with this!"

**SPEED 2:**
*CRUISE CONTROL*

STORY BY
JAN DE BONT AND RANDALL MCCORMICK

SCREENPLAY BY
RANDALL MCCORMICK AND JEFF NATHANSON

NOVEL BY
GEORGE RYAN

HarperPaperbacks
*A Division of HarperCollinsPublishers*

## HarperPaperbacks
*A Division of* HarperCollins*Publishers*
10 East 53rd Street, New York, N.Y. 10022-5299

This is a work of fiction. The characters, incidents, and dialogues are products of the author's imagination and are not to be construed as real. Any resemblance to actual events or persons, living or dead, is entirely coincidental.

ISBN 0-06-101257-2

HarperCollins®, ![logo]®, and HarperPaperbacks™ are trademarks of HarperCollins*Publishers* Inc.

Insert photos © Ron Phillips

Cover photo: tk

First printing: June 1997

Printed in the United States of America

Visit HarperPaperbacks on the World Wide Web at
http://www.harpercollins.com/paperbacks

❖ 10 9 8 7 6 5 4 3 2 1

"Be back in an hour," her friend said, leaving Annie Porter with her yellow Volkswagen Beetle in the parking lot of the Department of Motor Vehicles.

"See you," Annie said.

Her friend, who had been downsized the previous week, had volunteered to drive Annie here for the driving test the judge had insisted she pass before having her driving license restored to her. The suspension of her license was a result of a series of misunderstandings, bad timing, and plain bad luck, much too complicated to go into. It could have happened to anyone, she told herself, especially someone like herself, who was usually in a hurry. Other people had fewer things to do and led more laid-back lives. Here she was in Los Angeles, running around in a constant frenzy, just as if she were living back East, where everyone was always in a frenzy. After today, when she would pass her test and get her license back, things would be different. She would be in control. She promised herself that.

Feeling a bit anxious, Annie got out of the car to stretch her legs. She was in her twenties, a cute, perky brunette with big brown eyes and a generous mouth that often wore a big smile. Her shapely body was clad in a yellow midi, white slacks, and yellow sandals. She carried her summonses, court orders, suspended license, and department paperwork in triplicate in a little black Mossino backpack with a lot of zippers.

Annie was losing a full day's work for this, because her boyfriend dropped her off at work in the morning and a coworker brought her home in the evening. She didn't want to take a chance driving there herself without a license—not with her luck. Today, after the test, she and her friend would have lunch and go shopping. Or they might drop by the beach at Venice, so Annie could say hello to her boyfriend, who was a cop on the boardwalk there. It might be nice to surprise him. He'd recognize her car.

But first, she had to take the test. Perhaps it wouldn't be so bad today. Last week's test was something she was not going to think about now. It could have happened to anybody. The man giving her the test had been very nice about it. She remembered that he'd also listened sympathetically to things about Jack, her previous boyfriend, whom she had met that awful day when she was on the bus because her license was suspended. She would never have met Jack, or been on that bus, if the judge hadn't been so unreasonable about her license. Mr. Kenter was the inspector's name. She'd asked for him again today. Having someone she knew, even slightly, give her the driving test was going to be a big help.

Why was she pacing like this? She was not going to be nervous, she told herself, and got back in the car.

It was a clear, cool day in Los Angeles. Bob Kenter left the Department of Motor Vehicles office building and headed for the parking lot section where he met with driving test candidates. In his fifties and balding, Bob wore a short-sleeved sport shirt and khaki pants. He'd been worried about his health lately. Not that there was anything particular wrong with him, but everywhere he looked he seemed to see ads for medical problems or reminders that he ought to take better care of himself. Well, this morning he felt invigorated. He'd done his relaxation exercises and eaten a healthy breakfast. Clipboard in hand, he strode briskly into the parking lot. And then he saw the yellow VW Beetle.

It was the same one as last week, he was sure of that, but how could she be back so soon? How could she even still be alive? He glanced at his clipboard. Annie Porter was her name. Pasting a courteous smile on his face, he slowly walked toward the little yellow car.

She was sitting behind the wheel and gave him a big smile.

Bob remembered very well how she looked. He opened the passenger door and said, "Annie, you're back again—and so soon."

"I hope you don't mind, Mr. Kenter," she said, "but I requested you. I wanted to make up for last week."

He winced at the memory. "Why should I mind?" he asked insincerely, and then added, this time trying to fool himself, "I'm sure it will go much better today."

Bob lowered himself into the seat beside her and closed the door. While he was still adjusting his seat belt, he was thrown backward as the VW took off as if Annie were doing a standing start for the measured mile in a Funny Car hot-rod championship meet. They were leaving the parking lot at high speed when a Santa Monica bus zoomed by in the roadway directly in front of them. Annie braked in time to avoid running into its side. The safety belt saved Bob from hitting his head on the windshield.

Annie glanced at him. "Sorry, Mr. Kenter," she said, "but that bus was going too fast!"

"Yeah, yeah," Bob gasped. "Make a left here."

She flew along quiet, residential streets in Venice, driving casually and confidently. Her hands barely touched the wheel as the car hugged a tight corner at forty miles per hour.

Annie was telling Bob about her new boyfriend. "It's the little things that I'm still getting used to," she said. "If I drop my napkin in a restaurant, Alex will give me his. He opens my car door, he yells at my neighbors for me." She looked across at him. "He watches the videos I pick out."

Bob was clutching his kneecaps and staring straight ahead through the windshield. "Annie," he instructed, "slowly merge into—"

She slashed the car into the turning lane and went on, "My last boyfriend, Jack, wasn't exactly the romantic type. For my birthday two years ago, he bought me pepper spray. I thought it was perfume—and ended up in the emergency room." She added thoughtfully, "Relationships based on extreme circumstances never work out."

"Right," Bob agreed absently. He was watching for traffic.

"Right?" Annie asked, puzzled.

Bob nodded, realizing too late that almost any other word in the dictionary might have been better to use at that moment.

Annie was determined not to miss this right turn. She ruthlessly jagged the yellow Bug across two lanes—and cut off a truck. The truck slammed on its brakes. The plate-glass store windows held in frames on its sides slithered forward and shattered on the street.

"You okay?" Annie asked Bob, who had crumpled into a near fetal position to prepare for impact. "We usually make a *left* there."

"Jeez, Annie!" he moaned, unfolding himself into an upright position again. He was trembling. "We'll forget it," he offered. "Let's start over. Keep going ahead."

She drove on, picking up speed as she gained confidence once more.

With his hands on the dashboard Bob asked her tensely, "Annie, does your boyfriend drive like this?"

She turned to him, smiling nervously. "Alex?" she queried. "No, my Alex drives a ten-speed bicycle."


High in the Hollywood Hills, a truck was traveling so fast it was barely making the turns on the narrow, winding two-lane road. The truck was being chased by a motorcycle ridden by Officer Alex Shaw, a member of the Los Angeles Police Department SWAT team, and two police cars.

Wearing a black ballistics vest with the big letters LAPD on the back, but no helmet, and chewing gum, Alex talked into the radio on his neck as he drove. "He just came over the top of Hillside," he shouted, "heading for the Hollywood outlet." In his twenties, Alex was strikingly handsome, with dark hair, clean-cut features, and a muscular body of medium build.

"He's not going to make it, Alex, we're all set up," Mac's voice came back to him over the radio. A fellow SWAT team member, Mac was standing a few miles down the hill by a roadblock consisting of three police cars and a van. He came back on the radio to Alex, "Just be careful, you may see some traffic up there."

"Thanks," Alex acknowledged.

It was only a few moments before he came around a bend fast and met two cars. They were traveling slowly, having just had a scary experience with the truck. Alex brushed his shoulder on the first car but managed to avoid them both. The cars had pulled to the side by the time the two police cars flashed by them. Neither driver moved forward for another five minutes.

The truck was having some bad speed wobbles. Alex guessed that the stolen merchandise was shifting around in the back, making the vehicle even harder to steer. He could catch glimpses of the driver watching him in the truck's driver side mirror. Alex knew the perp would swing over to crush him if he tried to pass. Hell, the roadblock was ahead, and that would surprise this jerk. He should just stay behind and keep the pressure on the guy, if he ever got as far as the roadblock . . . which looked kind of doubtful, the way the truck body was bouncing around on the road surface.

It had started out as a regular alarm for breaking and entry into an office building, and ended as a call for the SWAT team when the clowns looting the offices thought they could shoot it out with the cops and make a getaway. The others were all trapped in the building, but this one had been loading stolen goods into the truck when the cops first arrived, and he ducked down out of sight in order to bide his time for an escape opportunity. Alex and his buddies had arrived at the scene before the guy made a break for it. He'd started the engine, shoved the truck in gear, and put his foot down hard on the gas.

An onlooker had run his motorcycle up onto the sidewalk to get a better view of the real life cops-and-robbers show. Alex "borrowed" the bike from him and took off after the fleeing truck. Running lights and weaving in and out of traffic, they had miraculously made it up into the hills without killing or maiming anyone. On the way, they picked up the two police cars, which were having a hard time keeping up. Alex had kept Mac and the other team members posted on his location, which gave them the chance to position a roadblock. All he had to do now was hang in, he told himself, and they would nail this maniac.

Alex was only fifty feet or so behind the truck when he thought he saw one of its back doors open. It wasn't his imagination. The door opened some more and computers and monitors came spilling out. A monitor hit the road ahead of him, bounced up and whistled past his ear, turning slowly on its axis, like it was in space orbit. Then the second door swung open, disgorging the contents of the truck.

Alex saw a boulder slide of computer equipment less than twenty yards in front of his bike. There was no way through this mess. The stuff was hitting the road and rolling in all directions. He realized if he hit one of them with his front wheel, he'd go head first over the handlebars without a helmet. As a cop, he knew what that looked like.

His peripheral vision somehow caught a gap in the safety rail over the canyon, and, on a split-second reflex he sliced through the gap. He kicked down a gear and struggled to control the bike on the dirt shoulder above the steep slope into the canyon. Then he twisted hard on the accelerator, determined to stay in sight of the truck.

The first police car tried to steer around the computers but didn't have a chance. The office equipment stove in the radiator, smashed the headlights, cracked the windshield, and damaged the bodywork. The second police car got away with just a few dents. The cops cursed and nosed their cars through the scattered computers. By the time they got through, however, the truck and motorcycle were long gone.

"Alex, what's your position?" Mac called over the radio.

On the wrong side of the safety rail, Alex was

having trouble keeping the bike from plunging into the canyon. As he tore along through weeds and dirt, the bike's tires were often only a couple of inches from the rim of the incline. Since Mac wanted to know, one word described his position. Desperate!

When he got a chance, Alex shouted into the radio, "I can't talk right now!"

That would have to do. He needed to concentrate on some serious steering. And only just in time. A hundred yards ahead, where the road started to turn, the dirt shoulder came to an end. Only the safety rail separated the roadway from the open canyon.

Just before the shoulder ended, there was a narrow gap in the rail. But he was traveling too fast. There was no way he could get through and back onto the road. The gap was too narrow. He leaned out into the canyon as far as he could without toppling over and threw his shoulder down in the opposite direction, taking the bike into the gap. The rail scraped the gas tank on one side and nicked against the footrest on the other.

He was back on the road again.


Bob Kenter looked at Annie Porter in confusion. He asked unbelievingly, "Alex . . . is . . . another cop?"

"I know, I know! No way would I ever date another cop after Jack," she said. "But Alex is so different. He works beach patrol, spends most of his time on a bicycle down in Venice. That's how we met. I was jaywalking."

"Jaywalking is a crime, Annie," Bob said with mock seriousness. "Make a left here."

"It's our anniversary tonight," she said, as the VW began to climb into the hills. "Seven months! Neither one of us has ever dated longer. So we're celebrating tonight, just in case—"

"Dip!" Bob warned.

Annie sped across a deep channel in the roadway designed to carry runoff rainwater and slow traffic. The VW's suspension was rigid to the point of being nonexistent, and the shaking they took would have turned your average surfer pale. Bob banged his head against the inside of the car roof. Annie didn't seem to notice.

"I'm not saying everything is perfect," she was saying. "We're still getting to know each other."

Bob heard police sirens in the distance. "Why don't you slow down and tell me your problems?" he suggested. As the sirens got a little louder, he nervously looked around.

"There's no problem. It's just that Alex can be a little quiet sometimes. He never talks about work . . . or how he's feeling."

"Well, that sounds like a nice, normal guy," Bob said, a bit puzzled. "Take my advice. Don't rush him."

•  •  •

Alex's motorbike was almost airborne as he tore downhill. The truck was no longer in sight. To gain on it, he wrestled with the bike and wrenched a performance from it like it had never been built to deliver. He leaned so far into corners as he took them at speed, his footrest scraped the tar surface of the road and his shoulder brushed dust from the roadside embankments.

Nearly a mile ahead of him two women on horseback struggled to control their mounts at the side of the road after a truck traveling at unbelievable speed frightened the animals. The horses were still snorting and prancing when they heard the approaching drone of the motorbike, sounding like a demented giant bee. The horses' eyes widened with fear and they flared their nostrils and did a nervous little dance. As the bike flashed past them, the horses reared and threw their riders.

Meanwhile, up ahead, the truck rounded a corner at high speed and the driver saw the van and three police cars forming the roadblock. He slammed on the brakes. The tires burned rubber as the truck spun 180 degrees, facing back the way it had come.

The SWAT team members steadied their rifle barrels on the car roofs and sighted in the scopes.

"Hold your fire!" Mac commanded. "He's too far!"

At this range, there were bound to be wild shots, the kind that could travel a half mile and kill some kid playing with a dog in his backyard.

The truck driver punched the gas and started heading back up the hill.

"Let's move!" Mac shouted.

The men jumped in their cars and took off after the truck. Nobody thought of radioing Alex.

Alex was still making his crazy downhill journey in hope of catching up with the truck, unaware that by now the truck was speeding uphill against him. He turned a corner and could hardly believe his eyes when he saw, at the end of a short straightaway, the hood of the truck straddling the center line of the two-lane highway and coming straight at him. They were no more than a hundred yards apart.

"Shit!" Alex said.

The truck driver smiled—or maybe it was a snarl. "Come on!" he ground out.

They were now only fifty yards apart. Alex had no choice. He turned the bike sharply and let the machine slide out from under him. He tried to relax his body as he came down on his back, hitting the road surface hard. Alex slid on his back across the tar like it was ice. His head was still on his shoulders, but he wasn't sure about anything else. He slid almost twenty feet and came to a stop in soft dust on the road side of the safety rail.

The smile froze on the truck driver's face as he saw that the downed bike was sliding into his speeding vehicle.

"Son of a—" He had no time to finish, being too busy twisting the steering wheel to avoid the bike.

He twisted the wheel a bit too far, and the truck spun out of control. It hit the bike and then crossed the road, missing Alex's prone body by an arm's length before hitting the safety rail.

The driver managed to open the door and jump out as the truck broke through the rail and suddenly vanished from sight down the steep slope of the ravine. It sounded like an empty tin box as it bounced and turned end over end on its way down. There was one final crunch far below and silence. Or near silence, because the engine of the mangled motorbike was still running and its rear wheel was spinning as it lay on its side in the middle of the road.

The driver of the truck rolled to a stop about three feet away from Alex. The two men looked at each other, hardly able to move. The driver tried to get up and screamed with pain.

Alex tried to find his own gun but couldn't. Lying where he was, he said to the driver, "You have the right to remain silent . . ."

Annie first heard sirens behind her and then saw police cars, their lights flashing, in the rearview mirror.

"Oh, shit," she said, "they can't be after us."

Along this stretch, the two-lane road was narrow, and on the right side there was a cliff.

"Pull over, Annie," Bob told her. "Can't you hear the sirens?"

"I *can't* pull over," Annie said, feeling panicky. The narrow road, the cliff right next to her, the cops with loud sirens and flashing lights pressuring her from behind . . . she didn't know what to do.

Bob was beginning to get seriously upset. "You already have six moving violations, not including speeding," he said. "Stop right here, Annie!"

She looked down at the cliff alongside and shuddered. The sirens were now so loud, she could hardly think. She put her foot down hard, and the little yellow Beetle put space between it and the two cop cars.

"Miss"—the voice came over the leading police car's rooftop speaker—"move over to the side, please."

"Where?" Annie shouted back in frustration. "There's a cliff!"

With relief, she saw a traffic sign for a T-junction ahead. She'd hang a right, and hopefully the two cop cars would turn left. She made a screeching right turn. Unfortunately, the two police cars did too, staying close behind her and sounding more urgent than ever.

"Annie, you didn't use your turn indicator!" Bob admonished her. He shook his head indignantly. "Can nobody operate a motor vehicle with responsibility anymore?"

They passed two women with dirt marks on their clothes who seemed to be trying to calm two horses. From the corner of her eye, as she swept by, Annie saw the horses rearing up on their hind legs and the women hanging on to their reins.

Mac pulled up in the SWAT van and looked out the side window at Alex, lying on the road looking fairly beat-up. But by now he'd found his gun and he was pointing it at the suspect, lying next to him. The perp was whimpering steadily, and every time he tried to move, he screamed with pain. Alex was looking like he might put a slug in him anyway.

Members of the SWAT team handcuffed the suspect, frisked him, read him his rights, and helped him into a police car. Mac left the van and casually walked around Alex, lying on the road. Mac looked over the safety rail into the canyon below, from where he could hear car horns blaring. The truck had tumbled down the slope onto a freeway in the bottom of the canyon, and now traffic was backed up for miles.

"Congratulations, Shaw," Mac said to Alex. "You just made a lot of new friends on the highways of Southern California. By the way, you are officially on vacation as of right now."

"Thank you," Alex said and tried to get up, but couldn't.

They both turned their heads toward the sounds of approaching police sirens. A yellow VW Beetle was coming at them fast, with two police cars close behind.

"What do they want?" Annie practically sobbed, clutching tightly on the steering wheel. "Oh, my God, I need my license back, Mr. Kenter."

Bob, as usual, was devoting his attention to the road ahead, and saw before she did the two police cars blocking it. "Stop, Annie, stop!" he yelled.

Annie looked ahead to see what was bothering

him, then slammed her foot on the brake. The yellow Beetle left burnt rubber tracks on the asphalt and then slid sideways to a stop right next to Mac's SWAT van. The Beetle was parallel parked so close to the van, Bob could not open his door.

"Nice driving, miss," a cop standing nearby remarked, impressed by her confidence with such close tolerances.

Inside the car, Bob looked across at Annie. His face wore an expression of sorrow and despair. "Annie," he said gravely, "you'll never drive in this town again."

Mac helped Alex to his feet and he hobbled over, clearly trying to hide his pain. As soon as Annie saw him, she jumped out of the VW and ran to meet him. They kissed.

"Did you pass your driving test?" he asked.

"Alex, what are you . . . ?" She was surprised to see him up here in the hills instead of down on the beach. Now she noticed that he was hurt. "What happened?" she asked.

"There's a perfectly reasonable-sounding explanation for this mess," Alex said in what he plainly thought was a soothing tone.

Another cop walked by and said, grinning, "You're a madman, Shaw. Nice working with you, as always."

Alex avoided Annie's questioning gaze.

.   .   .   .   .

For a TV newscast, a reporter stood talking in front of a video camera. Annie listened.

"So far, they have recovered some of the stolen computers," the reporter was saying, "and at least one member of the gang of robbers has been apprehended, thanks mainly to SWAT team member Alex Shaw, who was the injured officer in today's high-speed chase . . ."

Annie walked over to where a medic was cleaning Alex's wounds. "You lied to me!" she yelled at her boyfriend.

"Annie, I—"

"You never said you were on the suicide squad."

"I was going to tell you when we first met," Alex said, "but after hearing all those horror stories about Jack—how he was always getting hurt, how you thought he was crazy and you would never date anyone like that again—I decided to wait." He shrugged and smiled warmly at her before adding, "I didn't want to lose you."

Annie held her ground. "When did you plan to tell me?" she asked.

"Well . . . this seems like a good time," he said brightly. "I didn't plan it exactly—but I can be spontaneous."

"A spontaneous jerk! Look at you!" Annie was not softening. "Every day I've been picturing you down at the beach busting teenage pickpockets, helping old ladies cross the street, drinking lemonade!"

Annie turned on her heel and walked away from

him, her eyes brimming with tears. Her dreams of Alex as a smiling cop with a ten-speed bicycle were dashed on the cruel rocks of today's reality. He was just another maniac—maybe even worse than Jack, if that was possible. Only now was she beginning to understand the depths of Alex's deception. A SWAT team member trying to pass himself off as a nice beach cop! But now, at long last, the sordid secret of his hidden life was revealed!

Leaving the exasperated medic behind and trailing a length of bandage, Alex followed her down the road.

"Annie, listen!" he called. "Sometimes I *do* fill in for a friend of mine down there, and I often enjoy a glass of lemonade—"

"I feel like I don't even know you," Annie shot back at him over her shoulder. In a hurt voice, she said, "I don't understand. . . ."

Alex got in front of her and blocked her way. "Annie, you're right," he said. "We need to get to know each other. What if we go away together?"

"Oh, right. Where?"

"The Caribbean."

"The Caribbean?" She looked at him incredulously. "Do you have a concussion? We both work six days a week—we've never even gone away for a weekend."

Alex reached inside his ballistics jacket and produced two plane tickets. Annie took a step backward.

"A cruise," he said. "I was gonna surprise you tonight."

"This isn't fair," she objected. "You can't just pull out plane tickets and take me away to some island and make everything okay!"

"No, I'm not going to make it all okay. *We* are."

Alex took her hand and held it lightly until she looked him in the eyes. He waited a split second for her to withdraw her hand. When she didn't, he took her in his arms. Feeling her respond to his embrace, he kissed her softly, full on the lips.

"So," Annie said, extricating herself from his embrace, "when would we leave?" By the tone of her voice, she wanted to let him know she had not yet fully made up her mind.

"We're on the red-eye," he answered. "Just like my eyes will be if you say no. Red. From crying, Annie. Because, more than anything, I want us to—"

"Okay, cornball. Okay," she said. Then she gave him a big smile and went on, "We'll have a great time, won't we?"

Antigua's V.C. Bird Airport was surprisingly busy for such a small island, with all kinds of small planes taking off and landing on between-island hops. The immigration inspector hardly glanced at Annie's and Alex's passports, and the customs official waved them through with a welcoming smile, as if he'd known them all his life and was happy to see their familiar, honest faces. Here was a place that strangers were welcome, especially free-spending tourists from the large, wealthy nation to the north.

Annie and Alex walked their cart of bags through the automatic doors onto the sidewalk in front of the airport building. The early morning air was balmy and tropically fragrant.

Alex nodded to a large sign on a wall: SHUTTLE TO CRUISE SHIPS.

A row of buses waited, their doors open and engines idling. Annie froze when she saw them.

Steering their baggage cart toward the buses, Alex looked back at her and asked, "Annie, what's wrong?"

"I'm not into public transportation," she said, and spotted an approaching cab. "Taxi!" she shouted, and waved her arm.

The taxi pulled up beside them. A huge woman was squeezed behind the steering wheel, and calypso music played at high volume on the car radio. Alex put their bags in the trunk and they both sat in the backseat, holding onto anything they could as the cab sped through the countryside on the way to St. John's, the capital, supposedly six or so miles away. The countryside was flat. The driver told them that the many round stone towers they saw were what remained of old sugarcane mills. When they saw people playing cricket, she claimed that Antigua produced the best cricketers in the West Indies. They didn't argue. Anyway, Annie was too busy fantasizing about this woman driving Mr. Kenter around. She would have to leave him off at the emergency ward.

St. John's was a good-sized town, with a well-worn kind of cozy look. The streets were narrow, most of the buildings were made of wood, and many of the roofs were corrugated zinc. A lot of tourist stores had a T-shirt displayed that read:

*HURRICANE LUIS, YOU DANGEROUS, YOU FEROCIOUS, YOU TERRIBLE, YOU TOO DAMN WICKED!*

"Luis came in September, 'ninety-five," the driver said. "Those are only the polite words you can call him."

As the cab sped through the narrow streets on its way to the Deep Water Harbour Terminal, Annie seemed preoccupied with her thoughts, paying hardly any attention to the amazing skills and heart-stilling courage of their driver.

"Alex," she finally asked, "have you ever done this before?"

"What do you mean?"

"Well, living with someone . . . eating every meal with them . . . seven straight days, spending every minute together."

"No, never," he said. "Have you?"

"Not even close," she admitted. "You think we can do it? You think we can be a normal couple?"

"Annie," Alex said with a surprised smile, "we *are* a normal couple."

The taxi driver turned a corner and they saw the spectacle of the harbor in front of them—perfect blue water littered with huge sailboats, yachts, and cruise ship tenders. The taxi stopped in front of the tender for their cruise ship, the *Seabourn Legend.*


Annie and Alex handed over their bags and jumped onto the tender, which was moving gently on the calm harbor waters. The open boat was already crowded with passengers and their carry-on baggage. They couldn't find two empty seats together, so Annie sat in an open spot on the first bench and Alex headed for one on the rear bench.

"Take a seat, please, and we'll be on our way," a ship's officer in a white uniform called out. "Everyone take a seat."

Alex squeezed into the space next to a boisterous-looking couple, each about fifty pounds overweight and wearing matching FAT BUSTER T-shirts. It made him think about being packed like sardines in a can, except he was the sardine and they were two tunas. The tender pulled away from the dock.

"Just don't wedge me in so tight I can't break for the edge," the guy joked to Alex.

"Harvey's been known to get seasick on these little boats," the woman informed Alex.

"So," Harvey said, changing the subject, "is this your honeymoon?"

Alex shook his head and said, "No, not really, we're—"

"Oh, getting engaged then, eh?" Harvey asked, and went on without waiting for an answer, "It's a big step, my friend." He paused for a moment to think about it. "It's like jumping out of an open window fifty stories up. Splat! Game over! You drop like a dead bird."

"I'll keep that in mind," Alex said politely.

The hefty pair craned their thick necks to get a good look at Annie, on the first bench.

Feeling eyes on the back of her head, Annie turned around and saw the plump duo staring at her. The woman squealed her approval of Annie. Alex just shrugged.

Annie smiled vaguely, wondering what Alex had been saying to them, and turned forward again. She felt she could spend hours simply gazing at this beautiful harbor in the sunlight.

"First cruise?" a man seated next to her asked in a low voice.

Annie looked at him, hesitating for a second on how to react. He was of slim build and had a kind of lean and hungry look, with haunted eyes. His hair was brown and he was handsome in an offbeat way, with high cheekbones and sharp features. He was smiling at her pleasantly, harmlessly.

"Oh, yes," she said. "Yours, too?"

"Not by a long shot," he said quietly. Another smile. "Sorry, I'm John Geiger."

"Annie." She did not offer him her hand.

"I've gone on hundreds of trips like this," he said without a hint of boastfulness. "These cruise lines hire me to study their computer systems, how they interface with the real work environment."

"And so you search for problems?" Annie asked conversationally.

"Bugs," he corrected her.

"What if there's no bugs?" she asked.

"These are seven hundred million dollar ships," he said. "There's always bugs."

An awkward pause followed as neither of them could think of anything to say to the other. Annie eyed his carry-on bags—expensive leather cases that looked like they contained laptop computers and complicated electronic equipment.

"Doesn't seem like much of a vacation," she opined.

Geiger smiled. "Oh, it will be," he said. "This trip is going to be a blast."

The tender went out the mouth of the harbor then, and they both looked up at the towering white wall of the *Seabourn Legend*, all 55,000 tons of her anchored just outside the harbor.

Annie had heard that this was the most luxurious cruise ship in the world. It certainly looked like it from where she sat. At the back of the ship the marina doors were open and passengers were already snorkeling, jet skiing, and sunbathing on rafts.


Annie and Alex walked up the long, metal gang-plank from the tender into a door in the side of the huge ship. They were met by a photographer.

"Now this is a cute couple!" the man enthused, beginning his spiel of professional patter. "How about a picture? Don't move! Pictures don't move. What are your names?"

"He's Alex, I'm Annie."

"Alex and Annie! Adorable!" the photographer said in a patronizing tone. "Come on, a big smile for the newlyweds!"

Annie and Alex said together, "Actually, we're not—"

The flash popped. Annie and Alex looked at each other.

"That's only $34.50 for a double set of mugs," the photographer now said in a businesslike manner. "If you don't like a picture, return it for a photo credit on a future cruise. Welcome to paradise."

Annie and Alex followed their cabin steward, who seemed to be a perpetually happy type.

He led them down a staircase while telling them, "This ship boasts seven passenger decks, swimming pool, health spa, casino, dry cleaners, movie theater . . ."

They passed a huge ballroom, with a large banner over the bandstand: DIAMOND JEWELERS OF AMERICA CONVENTION. Down a hallway, they passed a bank office with a large vault secured by a heavy steel door.

"If either of you would like to put any of your valuables in the ship's vault . . ." The steward paused to look at them appraisingly. "Never mind," he said.

The man Annie had spoken to on the tender—

John Geiger—came along. "Did you find my golf clubs yet?" he asked the steward.

"Yes, sir," the steward answered. "I'll bring them up from storage as soon as the passengers are settled."

"Thank you." Geiger said. "Enjoy the cruise, everyone."

He smiled at Annie and climbed a staircase to an upper deck. Alex watched him go.

They descended another staircase. When they reached another passenger corridor and turned a corner, the steward pointed to a cabin door and announced dramatically, "In seven days you'll be sorry to leave room 6088, your happy home."

Alex pushed open the door, and he and Annie walked into the cabin. There were twin beds on each side. Annie pulled up the shade on the tiny porthole—and looked out at the side of a lifeboat.

"If you need anything at all, absolutely anything, *anything*, you just call Ashton." The steward tapped himself on the chest, in case they might think he was talking about someone else. "And let me thank you both in advance for the generous gratuity you will leave me at the end of the cruise." He grinned and added, "I'm just kidding."

"But not really," Alex said.

"No," Ashton agreed. "Have a nice honeymoon!"

Annie began, "Well actually, we're not ma—"

The door slammed behind Ashton, leaving Annie and Alex to stare about them at their humble cabin.

Turning to Alex with a smile and wrapping her arms around his neck, Annie said, "Thank you."

Their faces were just inches apart. Annie looked into his eyes and could see that his mind was racing. She had no idea what he might be uneasy about.

Looking distractedly past her around the cabin, he asked, "Is it big enough?"

"Size doesn't matter, you know," she said with a smile. They kissed, warmly and intimately. Then she went about unpacking her bag and arranging her things around the cabin.

While her back was turned, Alex urgently searched through his pockets.

"I don't know why," she was saying, busy unpacking, "I just got Love Boat fever. I'm suddenly all excited to be on a cruise. What's that about?"

He lifted his bag onto the other single bed, opened it, and quickly riffled through his things in a desperate search. As she turned to him, he hid his panic with a big smile.

"They must pump some drug through the air conditioning," she went on, going into the bathroom and leaving the door ajar. He dug into his bag again, as she continued, "I need lots of drinks with those little highly impractical umbrellas."

He found it! Taking a small jewelry pouch from his bag, he opened it to reveal an engagement ring. Alex put the ring on the tip of his pinky and stared at it. For one terrible moment, he had been sure he had forgotten it.

Music began to sound from an upper deck. It seemed to be party time up there. Annie came out of the bathroom, wearing a new outfit, and asked, "So who besides me is ready to party on a big boat?"

He stood there, awkwardly hiding the ring in his hand.

"You okay?" she asked, looking at him intently. "You seem a little tense."

"Me?" he responded, simultaneously deciding he was too nervous to pop the question right at this moment. "No, let's . . . uh . . . sure, let's go get a drink."

Following her to the door, he tried to pull the ring off his pinky. It was stuck!

"I have a feeling this trip's gonna be a blast," she said, going out the door.

"Yeah, I think you're right," he answered, managing to yank off the ring.


Captain Pollard arrived on the bridge of the *Seabourn Legend*. A physically fit man in his fifties, he looked handsome in his white uniform, with gold braid on the cap and epaulets. In his right hand he rotated two massage balls. The first officer and navigator, who were known to everyone as Juliano and Merced, respectively, sat in front of an impressive array of instruments. A detailed, three-dimensional computer model of the ship was displayed on an outsized monitor. When the captain approached the main computer, a computerized voice spoke: "Good morning, captain."

"Good morning," Pollard responded graciously.

Juliano hung up a phone receiver and said, "We're closing the marina, sir."

"Harbor patrol says go—we have all systems confirmed," Merced said. Handing the captain some papers, he went on, "These are the coordinates for the first leg, captain."

The captain took the papers and walked to one of the bridge windows. As far as he could see, the dark blue water stretched calm and unruffled beneath a paler blue, cloudless sky.

On the pool deck, a crew member used a chain saw to slice through a solid block of ice. He had already completed one ice sculpture, three feet high, of a dolphin standing on its tail as it rose out of the water. Sunbathing passengers with nothing else to do watched his sure strokes with the saw through the ice and tried to guess what he was making this time.

A band played calypso music by the pool. People danced, and a few threw streamers. One young couple were slow-dancing by the rail. On a TV set over the bar, two somber-looking jocks in suits and ties were doing a commentary on a golf tournament.

Carrying two giant multicolored drinks with little paper umbrellas stuck in them, Annie walked

toward Alex. At first he didn't notice her. He was
too busy being a cop, instead of a guy on vacation.
He was watching someone across the pool. Annie
followed his look.

"His name is Geiger," she said.

Alex turned around. "What?" he asked.

"He was sitting next to me on the tender," she
explained, and gave him his drink.

They both looked across the pool to the bar,
where Geiger sat on a stool pouring himself a cup
of hot tea. There were too many people and they
were too far away for Geiger to notice them looking
at him, although he was glancing at people around
him with a superior smile.

Alex said, "Yeah . . . he wanted his golf clubs in
such a hurry." He was thoughtful for a moment and
then said, "I don't think he golfs."

"Really?" Annie asked. "Why not?"

"The Players' Championship is on TV and he
hasn't even looked once."

"You're kidding me!" Annie gasped in mock horror. "You have to go arrest him right away!"

They both laughed and sipped on their brightly
hued drinks.

Suddenly Annie looked serious and took his
hand. "Alex," she said, "there's something I want
you to do for me—something I've never asked you
to do before."

"What?" he asked, looking a bit alarmed.

"I want you to boogie," she said.

Alex watched as she started to dance in front of him. He seemed to have a need to confirm her message. "You want me to boogie?" he asked.

"If you won't dance," she said, "just run in place next to me—move that butt a little."

At that moment, the cruise entertainment director rushed up. She had already introduced herself to them about four times as Liza. "Bingo! Bingo! Bingo!" Liza yelled with such urgency she made it sound like they'd just been torpedoed. "Just a reminder, tonight is bingo night in the Crystal Lounge! Your first two cards are on the house! You can't win if you don't play bingo, bingo!"

Thankfully, she rushed on without delay to another couple and began again with her bingo routine. When Alex glanced back across the pool, he found that Geiger had gone.

On the bridge, the captain watched as Juliano keyboarded instructions to the computer.

"Both engines are at fifty percent, sir," Juliano reported.

"Let's take her out," the captain said.

Only on the lowest decks could the vibrations of the two massive diesel engines be faintly felt as they powered the huge ship forward. The enormous twin propellers churned the surface of the water in the ship's wake. In a stately, dignified way, the gleaming white *Seabourn Legend* put out to sea.

. . .

Wearing a raspberry-colored bikini with a high-cut leg, Annie lay on a deck chair, soaking in the sun in a quiet corner on the pool deck, away from the main social action. Alex was swimming in the pool. She intended to enjoy some restful peace and quiet. She literally couldn't remember the last time she'd been able to just lie back and relax, without something that urgently needed to be done or some friend who had to be helped through a crisis or broken heart. There was no telephone here. She did not have to be anyplace by any particular time. That awful driving license mess—but no, she was not going to think about that . . . No one had to drive anywhere on a ship. She was going to do something for herself for a change, self-indulgently take some precious time for her own pleasure. Time she did not have to devote to someone else, no matter how deserving. Simply lying there and thinking that she didn't have to think about anything was a joy in itself. Beside the chair, she had everything she could possibly need—sun block, diet soda, a couple of magazines, and a paperback mystery.

She'd gotten some sleep on the overnight plane from L.A. to Miami, but then of course they had arrived at the airport in Florida at some incredible hour with the sun only beginning to peep over the horizon and the first birds waking—no, there were no birds. Then they had to find the small airline with a name no one seemed to have heard of. After they found the gate, at the end of endless corridors, out near the Everglades, she had to worry whether their bags would be transferred. If the bags missed that flight to Antigua, they wouldn't be on the cruise ship with them. Alex wasn't worried—he wouldn't mind spending a week in the same pair of jeans and T-shirt with no razor. . . . They made their connections, the bags arrived, the ship sailed, there were no hitches—and now she was exhausted.

Her mind was still racing. It would be a couple of days before she calmed down and could fully relax. But right now, this was bliss. There was nothing more that she could ask for. Shine on, sun. Sail on, ship. This was how other people lived. She wanted Alex to see that. Other couples weren't always caught up in crazy stuff like they were, rushing here and there, often not having time for one another for days on end. That was no way to live. Alex was the sort of man who could understand that. Unlike Jack, who used to get nervous when he wasn't in the middle of a fire, mudslide, or a homicide. Learning that Alex was a SWAT team member had been a shock. But she was sure that once he got a chance to do some normal living, Alex would develop a taste for it. This cruise might make all the difference.

On a cruise like this, a couple might find together the tranquility that eludes so many people in the modern world. Annie had seen a man on late night cable who explained it all. She hadn't been able to find a pen to write down the 1–800 phone number, but even so, she felt she'd learned a lot from listening to him and some of the people whose lives he had transformed. How exactly it worked, she'd forgotten, but she was not going to let details like that prevent Alex and her from transforming their lives. She liked those words. Right now, as she lay there in the sun on the gentle sea, she felt that she might be transforming her life. Of course, you couldn't be sure—you could only tell afterward whether you had done so or not.

She sensed a large shape blocking out the sun then—much too big to be Alex. With mild irritation, she took off her sunglasses and looked up at Harvey, the man who'd spoken to her on the tender. He was still wearing the FAT BUSTER T-shirt. He was also holding two ice cream cones, one of which he was licking. The other was dripping onto the covers of her magazines.

"I brought this for you," he said, and held out the melting ice cream cone to her.

She took it, only because if she hadn't, the cone would have dripped on her too.

"You and your boyfriend, Debbie and me, are all at the same table for dinner each night, Debbie arranged it," he said, apparently thinking Annie would be pleased at this news. "We're not far from the captain's table."

Holding the sticky, rapidly dissolving ice cream

at arm's length from her body, Annie said the only thing she could think of: "Where's Debbie?"

Harvey pointed with his ice cream cone. "Over there," he said.

Annie didn't bother to look. My God, she thought, were these people going to attach themselves to her for the entire trip? She would have to tell Alex. He would know what to do with them. There was nothing wrong with them as people. She just didn't want to be with them. And why her? Why had they selected her? Was there something about her that drew needy people to her? Only a minute ago she'd been thinking about living tranquilly with Alex—and now here was Harvey blocking the sun, and ice cream was trickling over her fingers!

Thankfully, Harvey didn't seem to have anything more to say to her and seemed content to simply stand there, keeping the sun's deadly gamma rays away from her skin.

Debbie showed up a few minutes later, wearing her matching T-shirt and digging with a plastic spoon into a half-gallon paper tub of ice cream. She looked critically at the sagging cone in Annie's hand. "Wrong flavor?" she inquired.

"I'm not in the mood," Annie said.

"Then dump it in here," Debbie said, extending her tub.

Annie did. She also took the paper napkin Debbie offered and wiped the ice cream from her hand. Pieces of napkin tissue adhered to Annie's skin. Two of her fingers were stuck together. She poured diet soda over them. This was not how she'd imagined a cruise on the world's most luxurious pleasure ship.

Debbie was chomping down on pieces of cone along with her own ice cream in the tub. "Get out of the sun, Harvey," she said. "You know it fries you to a crisp."

Harvey only shrugged his meaty shoulders.

"He was a roofing contractor, but he had to give it up," Debbie said to Annie.

"Because of the sun?" Annie asked.

"It was New Jersey," Harvey said. "Ice was more of a problem than sun."

"That was during our first marriage," Debbie said, a dreamy look coming into her eyes. "Remember then, Harvey?"

"Yeah, doll, you were great."

"Your first marriage?" Annie prompted.

"Yeah, we got divorced," Debbie said. "We were incompatible."

Harvey nodded in confirmation. "We were young," he explained. "We never agreed on anything. Each of us always thought we were in the right."

"Later we discovered we were usually both wrong," Debbie said.

"So we had something in common after all," he added.

"You got married again?" Annie asked.

"After he quit the roofing," Debbie said. "By then he was selling heavy machinery in Orange County. I came west for a cousin's graduation at UCLA and decided to look up this lug while I was in the neighborhood. I never got back to New Jersey, after telling the people I worked for I'd be away three days."

Annie laughed. Maybe dinner wouldn't be so bad after all. "Harvey," she said, "mind giving me a little sun?"

4

That night, Geiger retrieved the golf bag from the closet where Ashton had placed it. He carefully inspected the bag and clubs for any signs of tampering. Satisfied that nothing had been interfered with, he emptied the clubs from the bag, turned it upside down and unscrewed the end of the bag. He had trouble with this. Finally he got the end of the bag off and removed handfuls of golf balls wrapped in plastic.

Next, he unscrewed the head of the driver. From the hollowed-out head of the club, he extracted miniature electronic timers, detonators, and coils of thin, differently colored wires.

He pulled a chair into the middle of the room,

climbed up on it and removed a panel from the ceiling. Exposed inside the ceiling were loose bundles of variously colored wires and optic fibers running in several directions. Geiger searched among them for certain ones, and as he found them, a look of satisfaction spread across his face.

Over two hundred well-dressed passengers sat at tables in the festively decorated dining room. A reggae band played while waiters cleared plates from the main course and others brought in trays heaped with desserts.

Annie and Alex shared a table with Harvey and Debbie, who were no longer wearing matching T-shirts, and the Fisher sisters—Fran and Ruby—Texas born and bred. At an adjacent table a pretty girl of about fourteen sat with her parents, Celeste and Rupert. With them were a dignified couple, Constance and Frank. Next to them sat Isabel and Alejandro, young newlyweds from Spain who had been slow-dancing at the pool in the morning. Even at the table they were having trouble keeping their hands off each other.

Debbie, meanwhile, was having trouble keeping her hands off the food. She grabbed a whole trayload of desserts and more or less chased the waiter away. Annie and Harvey joined her in scooping up desserts and enjoying themselves. Alex seemed thoughtful, looking as if he wished he and Annie were alone.

Debbie waved a pastry to make her point. "The misconception is that fat is bad," she said, "that to *lose* fat you shouldn't *eat* fat. Guess what."

"False," Harvey said. "Your body is just a giant computer." He seemed to have heard this before.

Debbie nodded. "If you don't eat fat," she said, "your body's central mainframe goes, 'Whoa! Better keep whatever fat I've got!' So we at Fat Busters say, 'Fat is your friend!'"

"Not your best friend," Harvey warned.

"But a pretty good friend," Debbie said defensively.

"Hey, I need a friend," Alex said, suddenly brightening up.

"Well, meet this guy," Annie said, handing him a brownie. "Sign me up for your program," she said to Debbie. "I don't care what it costs."

Alex noticed that the young girl at the next table signed to her mother in American Sign Language. Only now did he realize that she was handicapped. The mother signed back, speaking as she did so, presumably because the girl could read lips too.

"One dessert!" her mother said, signing rapidly. "*One*. I don't care *what* the lady says."

Alex guessed the girl had lip read Debbie's message to humanity. Both he and Harvey looked as a man at another table noisily dropped a fork on his plate, rose unsteadily to his feet and hurried off.

"Mal de mer," Harvey diagnosed. "First night's always the worst. Remember, Deb?"

Debbie looked as if she would prefer not to. The band finished a number and got some applause. Isabel and Alejandro were all over each other once more. The microphone squealed. It was Liza again, this time on the bandstand, calling for everyone's attention.

"Ladies and Gentlemen," she said in her singsong, penetrating voice, "I have a question. Who would like a peek at a multimillion-dollar jewelry collection?" She waited for applause and got some. "Well, on board we've got the Diamond Jewelers of America with us tonight, and they'd like to show you something." This time the applause was louder.

The band played another tune as five gorgeous models sashayed among the tables, wearing big solitaire stones and carrying display cases lined with sparkling earrings, bracelets, and necklaces. The diamonds sparkled and blazed in the spotlights, and photographers' flashbulbs turned the stones into icy flame for a millisecond.

Fran couldn't take her eyes off them. "Diamonds . . ." she gasped in a strangled voice. She was almost in a trance.

"No touching, Fran," her sister cautioned.

"But look at the diamonds . . ."

"Fran!" Ruby said sharply.

At the next table Frank sat back, enjoying both the models and the diamonds, while Constance nervously sipped coffee. He beamed at his newly smoke-free wife and said, "Maybe we should get you a little something."

"I'll take a Camel, unfiltered," Constance snapped.

"Honey, aren't you wearing the nicotine patch?"

Irritated now, Constance replied, "The only way that patch is going to help is if I roll it and *smoke* it!"

The young girl looked longingly at some pastries. She turned her back on her mother and this time tried signing to her father. He signed back to her, with a firm look on his face. She pushed her plate away and folded in her arms in disgust.

To Annie's—and the young girl's—amazement, Alex began signing to her. At first the girl watched him sulkily, but then she smiled at something he communicated to her. She unfolded her arms and signed back to him.

During a break in their silent conversation, Annie said to Alex, "That's impressive."

"I'm just making it up," he told her jokingly. "Her name's Drew." As he and the girl continued to sign, he translated for Annie. "She wants to know if you're my sister."

"Let her down easy," Annie recommended.

"She says you're very beautiful," Alex continued, "and that your kids will be beautiful too."

Annie smiled sweetly at Drew and said, "Thank you."

Drew smiled back.

Drew had given Annie something to think about. "Jeez, picture me as a mom," she mused aloud.

"You're going to make a beautiful mother," Alex assured her. "Just don't drive carpool."

"Kids . . . I don't know," Annie went on dreamily. She pulled herself together. "I'd just love a chance to finish my dinner first."

Debbie was interested. Her upper lip was smeared with cream as she looked closely into Annie's face and asked, "What? Kids aren't on the menu?"

"Oh, they're on the menu," Annie replied coolly. "It just depends who's ordering."

As a model showed a huge solitaire in a display case to Isabel and Alejandro, distracting nearly everyone's attention, Alex moved closer to Annie for a private moment together. Glancing at a tray of engagement rings, he asked, "So, can you order a la carte?"

Playing it safe, Annie decided to go along with the role of waitress. "See, I don't know if you're sitting in my section," she said.

"Yeah," he said. "I requested your table."

"Well, are you a good tipper?" she asked.

"Depends on the service."

"It's always service with a smile for you," she said.

She looked in his eyes.

He didn't appear to be joking anymore.

"Are you being serious?" she asked.

"Maybe . . ." he mumbled.

Was he changing his mind? Why wouldn't he

just say it? Her mind tumbled. *I can't believe this.*
She was speechless for several moments—and suddenly found her voice: "I . . . I mean I just found
out I'm dating a . . . you know . . . a *daredevil*. And
to make that kind of"—she picked up a pastry and
nervously bit into it—"that kind of commitment to
someone who basically, on a day-to-day basis,
jumps out of cars while getting shot at—I'm not
saying I don't have those feelings for you, but I definitely have, you know, feelings about your insane
occupation. I mean, what if you found out *I* was on
the bomb squad?" She tried to meet his eyes. "Oh,
wait . . . you're *not* serious, are you?"

"Annie . . ." He seemed choked up with emotion.

"What?"

After a long pause, he said in a small voice, "I'm
seasick."

"Huh?"

"Gonna throw up," he warned, getting to his feet
and looking nauseous.

Annie quickly stood and led him by his arm out
of the dining room.

Harvey sympathetically looked after them.


Geiger approached the engine room with a black
bag slung over one shoulder. He slid an ID card into
a security slot and the access door opened automatically. Huge steam turbines throbbed and hissed,
and vertical steel ladders led up to gratework

catwalks above his head. The farther he walked into
the engine room interior, the louder the engines
became. Their sound was nearly deafening at the
point where he heard two engineers shouting to one
another before he saw them. Geiger kept out of
sight and kept on walking until he spotted an emergency fire sprinkler high on one wall. The sprinkler
was located near a steel ladder. Placing his black bag
on the floor, he selected a foot-long jimmy from it
and climbed the ladder. It took only seconds for
him to pry the cap off the sprinkler. Water poured
out—not a torrent certainly, but enough to register
on the engineers' computerized troubleshooting
monitors.

Geiger jumped down off the ladder, picked up
the bag and hurried out of sight.

In less than a couple of minutes one of the two
engineers Geiger had seen was showing a flashing
red section of an electronic circulation plan to the
other.

"What's that?" he bellowed.

The other man shook his head to indicate he
didn't know. He beckoned for his colleague to follow, and they went to check it out.

"Oh, dammit," the one in front said when he
stepped in the growing pool of water beneath the
emergency sprinkler. They searched for the cap,
complaining about the careless workmanship of
others who had not attached it properly. They were
too occupied to come across Geiger, who, not far

away, had opened the emergency control box of one engine and was attaching wires to it from a small handheld computer with a miniature display screen.

To clear their heads after dinner, Annie and Alex took a walk on the muster deck. The stars looked huge in the sky above and were so bright they glinted on the waves. Yes, Annie realized, waves. A stiff night breeze had risen, and the ship rose and sank gently in the swells.

"Are you okay, Alex?" she asked. "You look a little pale."

"No, I'm fine," he claimed.

"We're on our first vacation, and you're uptight," she complained. "You start arguing about kids—"

"I'm not uptight," he snapped. "Just nervous, I guess," he allowed.

Annie didn't see what he had to be nervous about and she racked her mind for an explanation. "I read something once," she recalled, "they took these rats from a stress-filled environment, then bathed them in comfort and safety . . . and suddenly the rats' blood pressure hit the ceiling. They couldn't handle it."

"You're calling me a rat?" Alex asked with a smile.

Annie smiled too, but she pulled away a little as they walked. "No, we're just talking," she said.

"Pretending to be a normal couple. We never talk about anything, you know."

Alex stopped and turned to her. "Well, let's change that tonight," he said with finality. He reached into his pocket for the box that held the engagement ring he'd secretly bought for her.

She mistook his change of tone as a combative challenge to her. She struck back. "Okay," she retorted, "how did you get the stab wound on your shoulder?"

Alex wasn't expecting this and forgot momentarily about the ring. He mumbled, "It's not really a stab wound. . . ."

"Okay, we'll try an easy one," she said briskly. "What's your badge number?"

"It's . . ." He paused to think. "I think it starts with a four."

"What about the other women you've dated?"

"I don't remember their badge numbers either." He smiled warmly at her and said, "That's not what I want to talk about." He took the ring box from his pocket. "We've been together seven months now, and that's long enough for me to know that you're—"

The boat rose up on a big swell, pitched at an odd angle, and then the deck sank gently away beneath their feet. Alex stared into her eyes, saying nothing.

"What?" she asked impatiently.

"Annie . . . I really think that . . ." He put the ring

box back in his pocket. "I really think I'm gonna be sick."

He rushed to the rail and was about to put his head over it when Annie caught him by the arm.

"Alex, not there!" she said. "This way! You're against the wind!"

On the bridge, Merced, the navigator, rapidly keyboarded more data into the computer. Captain Pollard and Juliano, the senior officer, looked at the radar screen and satellite navigation and computer monitors. All three turned sharply when they heard a voice behind them.

"I must be lost," the man said in a slurred voice.

It was John Geiger, swaying slightly, his tie crooked and hair untidy.

"Sir, you can't be here right now," Juliano said.

Geiger looked like he might curl up someplace any moment and pass out. "I saw all the lights, thought this was the casino," he said thickly. "I could really use a drink. Any of you gambling men?" he asked hopefully.

Stepping closer to the computer, he slipped and almost fell, saving himself by clutching the back of a chair.

The captain steadied him by holding his upper arm and asked with icy politeness, "Sir, can we help you find your cabin?"

"I know where it is," Geiger said argumenta-

tively. "I know when I'm not wanted." He looked
at them and then peered out through a window at
the night seas. "You guys just watch where you're
going," he said, reminding them of their duty. He
made his way to the door and stumbled onto the
deck.

The captain and the two officers exchanged tolerant smiles. All three men had dozens of funny stories to tell about things that happened on cruises. If
you were the kind of person who took everything
very seriously, this was not the business for you to
be in. None of them noticed the small black transmitter that Geiger had stuck on the back of the main
computer.

While Geiger staggered his way to his cabin, Annie
lay wide-awake in her cabin, watching TV. Alex, on
his single bed, was out cold, his hand draped over
an ice bucket on the floor beside the bed.

Once inside his cabin, Geiger had an instanta-
neous return to cold sobriety and keyboarded data
into both his laptop and handheld computers.
Suddenly the voices of the officers on the bridge
sounded in the cabin in perfect stereo.

"Radar looks good," Merced said. "We should
have smooth sailing for the rest of the night."

"Switch us back to autopilot," Captain Pollard
ordered.

"That's right, switch us over," Geiger agreed,

grinning. "Take the night off, you're in good hands."

"Switching over . . . now," Merced announced.

Geiger sat back in an easy chair and reviewed the setup in his mind, with a smug expression on his face. On the back of the engine room autopilot control panel, he had attached a transmitter similar to the one on the bridge computer. A receiver for these two transmitters was wired to his laptop. The laptop, in turn, was wired to the communications system that ran through the ship in the space above ceilings. Geiger felt he had reason to be pleased with himself. So far, everything had gone without a hitch. This looked like it was going to be even easier than he'd anticipated.

He hit a few keys on the laptop and the screen went blank. Geiger rose from the chair and stood in front of the laptop. After a few seconds the same computerized voice that had greeted Captain Pollard on the bridge that morning sounded loud and clear: "Good evening, captain."

Geiger smirked and said out loud, "At least someone recognizes who's in charge here."

The sea air took its toll. Even those passengers who had not drunk or eaten too much, or who were not seasick or exhausted from dancing for hours, flopped down on their cabin beds and fell into a deep sleep. Insomniacs who claimed they hadn't had a wink of sleep for weeks snored in abandon. Those who prided themselves on being night people had long ago begun yawning in each other's faces, saying they could not figure out what was coming over them. Segments of the crew had unobtrusively gone off duty as the night owls became fewer in number. By two in the morning only the intrepid few remained. And even some of them had begun to stifle yawns . . .

At three A.M., Geiger left his cabin, with his black bag on one shoulder. In a corridor lined with passenger cabins, he used a screwdriver to remove the grill from an air-conditioning vent. He took one of almost two dozen golf balls in his bag and fiddled with an electronic device implanted in the ball. Then he carefully positioned the golf ball inside the vent and replaced the grill.

He spent until almost five in the morning locating the golf balls in strategic positions around the ship. When the radio officer left the radio room for a few minutes to fetch breakfast, Geiger slipped a golf ball behind the power supply control panel for all radio and satellite communications. He had given the occasional passengers and crew members he'd come across a cheerful good-night. Luckily, no one had seen him actually doing any "repairs." There had been no need for any explanations, and nothing unusual had occurred that might have raised questions in people's minds. Again, everything had gone so smoothly, it might have worried a lesser man than Geiger. But Geiger saw it as his due. At long last, things were starting to go his way.

Tired, he made his way back to his cabin. He stripped and ran himself a lukewarm bath. He helped himself to medications from a number of prescription bottles. Some were remedies for copper and heavy metals poisoning, and others were for chelation therapy. Then he picked up a large glass jar, three-quarters filled with water and containing slowly moving black objects. He lay in the water and carefully tested its temperature. When he judged it sufficiently cool, he said aloud, "Time for group therapy."

He reached into the jar and pulled out a squirming black creature. "Now this is decent treatment," he said. He spoke directly to the slimy creature writhing in his fingers: "I wouldn't trade you for any of my doctors."

He placed the leech on his chest and felt its mouth fasten on his skin. But he did not feel it puncture his flesh and begin to feed upon his blood.

One by one he removed the hungry leeches from their jar and applied them to his body. Finally, when the bloodsucking leeches were clinging tightly all over, he smiled down at them benevolently.

"You take care of me," he said to them. "I'll take care of the ship."

When Annie awoke, she found herself alone in the cabin. She looked at the clock. It was already 10:35.

"Alex?" she called, thinking he might be in the bathroom.

There was no response. She supposed he'd decided to let her sleep and quietly gone up on deck. She lay on her back on the bed, enjoying the luxury of not having to get up to be any particular place by any particular time. That was a vacation in itself.

There was a knock on the door. Without any delay or further warning, the door opened and Ashton entered carrying a tray.

"The love birds ordered breakfast in bed," he said with a big smile.

"Oh, yes . . ." Annie answered vaguely.

He placed the tray on the bedside table and was gone again in a few moments, apparently without having noticed that the cabin was one love bird shy.

The gleaming white ship sliced through calm blue-green seas, and the sun was beginning to come into its full midday power, tempered only by a gentle salty breeze. On the rear upper deck, Alex was skeet shooting. He was very fast and very accurate, nailing everything. Plainly, he was working off the frustration of being seasick the previous night. He felt himself again today and was happy to be able to prove it.

He pumped the shotgun and raised it to his shoulder. "Pull!" he shouted.

The bright yellow clay pigeon was thrown from the trap at an odd angle, imitative of the way a wild bird might take wing. Somewhere in the back of Alex's mind, the advice of an old coach sounded: overtake it, pass it at noon and squeeze. The clay pigeon disintegrated in midair.

A two-eye shooter, he had a broader field of vision than the majority of shooters, who were dominant in one eye and had to close the other while shooting. He pumped the gun again and prepared to shoot.

On a nearby deck chair, Drew read a magazine but looked up frequently to watch Alex shoot. In her eyes, Alex was easily the coolest guy on this ship.

On the deck above, Geiger was drinking coffee and picking at a late breakfast. He had not had as much sleep as he needed, and the shotgun blasts were having a bad effect on his nerves. All the same, he leaned over the rail and intently watched Alex shoot. Although Geiger's mouth wore a scowl of contempt, Alex's shooting brought a reluctant glint of respect to his eyes from time to time.

As Annie approached, Frank held his finger to his lips and whispered, "Constance is concentrating."

Annie had met the two of them last night. They were both tall, rail thin, and fastidiously polite to people other than themselves. Old-money WASPs from back East, Alex had remarked.

Wearing a royal-blue silk seat shirt and sweat pants, Constance was sitting in the lotus position on a mat, gazing in front of her with faraway eyes. "Hello, Annie," she said, without moving a muscle.

"Hush, dear," Frank said. "Remember, concentrate on *being there*."

"I *am* here, Frank," she said. "I don't have to concentrate. It feels like hell."

Moving away, Annie said, "I don't want to interrupt—"

"Stay!" Constance commanded. "I can't take much more of this."

Frank helped her to her feet, saying, "Perhaps it's time for a chardonnay."

"No, Frank. If I can't have a cigarette, you can't have a drink. Besides, it's still morning."

Annie noticed the beautiful material in Frank's rumpled gray sweatshirt and sweatpants. She was certain they were hand-tailored. Constance, in her silk outfit, makeup, and elaborate hairdo, clearly had no intention of perspiring. All three of them sat down at a table.

"Constance finally managed to quit smoking," Frank said. "That's what this trip is about. We're celebrating."

"My triumph over vice," Constance said.

"We're celebrating," Frank repeated.

"*You're* celebrating," she said. "It was bad enough quitting. Celebrating it all the time is even worse."

"You have a right to be proud of yourself," Frank protested. "What do you think, Annie?"

"I don't know," Annie said, wanting no part of this.

"Do you have a special reason for being on this cruise?" he asked her.

"Alex bought the tickets. A surprise."

"He's with a police department, isn't he?" Constance said. "Frank is in public relations in New York."

"For celebrities?" Annie asked.

"Our firm does that," Frank said, "but I work mostly with companies. Every time a company causes an oil spill or fires a lot of people who have worked for them for years, or gets caught bribing a politician—things like that—they need a public relations firm. We explain to the public how their initial impression was mistaken, how these really are nice people and it was all a mistake or accident that no one was responsible for. You'd be surprised how well P.R. works."

"I don't think it would work on me," Annie said.

Frank looked at her levelly. "I believe you're right," he said. "You know the people most easily influenced by P.R.?"

"Who?"

"People who think they know all about current events, who read and watch serious stuff. We can influence their minds easily, especially the ones who pride themselves on being independent thinkers."

"But you can't get to me?" Annie asked.

"We can't get to you," Frank agreed with a grin. "You don't pay any attention to us."

"I'd love a cigarette," Constance said.

"What do you work at?" he asked Annie, ignoring his wife's remark.

"Animal therapy."

Constance was interested. "Injured pets?" she asked.

"In a way," Annie said. "But we don't take in physically injured animals—they go to the vet. The animals we get mostly belong to people who travel a lot or are away from home for extended periods. Their pets often get lonely or upset at boarding kennels or other places. Sometimes they go crazy. That's when they start coming to us."

"Disturbed pets," Constance said. "What do you do for them?"

"Get to know them," Annie said. "They're just like people in that way. When you like them and pay heed to them, they start acting nice again."

"Even the crazy ones?" Constance asked.

"Most of them. Animals are simpler than people," Annie said. "When they're wild, you can tame them."

"Frank and I are tame."

"Alex is wild," Annie said and sighed.


Annie went to the swimming pool deck, hoping to find Alex splashing in the water or sunning himself beside it. Two men played steel drums by the crowded pool. There was no sign of Alex there. Under the shade of an umbrella, Debbie and Harvey sat at a table eating hot dogs.

"Have you guys seen Alex?" Annie asked.

"He wasn't at breakfast," Harvey answered. "Is he okay?"

"He got a little sick last night, but—"

"Oh, he did?" Harvey snickered. "Heh heh. Been there."

Annie quickly walked on.

As she was doing so, Alex was descending a spiral staircase into the ship's atrium. Finished with skeet shooting, he'd checked the cabin to see if Annie might still be asleep. Not finding her there, he thought he would look around for her. At first he thought he'd have no problem catching sight of her. Now it was dawning on him what a huge place this ship was, and how it might be possible for him to wander about all day, from deck to deck, without ever finding her. He passed the ballroom, where the jewelers' convention was in full swing. Through the open doors he could see models displaying large diamonds that sparkled with such power, they were dazzling from twenty feet away.

The ship's photographer was taking pictures of people entering and leaving the convention. As Alex approached, the photographer offered to take his picture. Alex waved him off his sales pitch and asked, "Is there any way to page somebody on the ship? I seem to have misplaced my girlfriend."

Celeste and Rupert were leaving the jewelers' convention showroom when they bumped into Annie. "Buy anything?" she asked them.

"We're plain Midwest folks, Annie," Rupert said. "Women don't wear big diamonds in Cincinnati."

"He means men don't give them to us," Celeste said, smiling. "We'd wear them, all right."

"How about you?" Rupert asked Annie.

"If people saw a cop's girlfriend wearing a big diamond, you know what they'd think," Annie said.

"So you keep yours hidden," he said.

"Yeah, right." As if it were an afterthought, Annie asked, "You haven't seen Alex, have you?"

"No," Celeste said. "When we do see him, we want to thank him for chatting to Drew in sign language. We never expected to meet someone on the cruise who could. You see, Drew has been going to camps for the hearing-impaired since she was little. Rupert and I decided it's time now for her to mix in the real world."

"Where does she go to school?" Annie asked.

"For the past two years she's been to our local regular school," Celeste answered. "Before that, she always went to special schools. She made the transition very well—Drew is able to stand up for herself."

"Her mother has always been very emotionally supportive of her," Rupert said fondly.

"Her father, also," Celeste said, returning his look.

Annie was touched. "You seem to be a very close, loving family," she said.

"We have our troubles, same as any other," Celeste said. "Plus an adolescent daughter."

"I remember what I was like," Annie said.

"Me too," Celeste added.

"We just wanted Drew to see what a cruise was like," Rupert said. "I suspect any thirteen-year-old girl—"

"She's fourteen," Celeste said.

"Any fourteen-year-old girl should be fascinated by a cruise," he said.

"At fourteen, I'd have been bored to death on a cruise," Annie said.

Rupert looked startled.

Celeste raised her eyes to the ceiling. "Rupert can't see why Drew doesn't want to play golf," she said.

"Anyway, I think you're right in having Drew lead as normal a life as possible," Annie said. "I'm trying to help Alex lead a normal life."

"Is Alex handicapped?" Rupert asked.

"No, no, not in that way," Annie said, sorry now that she'd opened her mouth about this. "What I meant was, how do I go about getting him to settle in for a quiet evening after a day of chasing bad guys?"

Rupert nodded. He said, "Like how does he go back to driving at fifty-five after doing eighty-five all day in his police car?"

"I'm the one who drives at eighty-five," Annie said.


Annie walked past a meditation class. Liza, the entertainment director, was leading it. Annie couldn't help hoping Liza would find some inner peace and tranquility from the meditation that would slow her down and make her less of a motormouth. But she had her doubts. Even meditation had limits.

They were all doing breathing exercises. Annie slipped away before Liza spotted her and tried to rope her in.

As she walked along a corridor, she heard a public address system right over her head mention her name. The voice of a woman who had clearly once had elocution lessons said: "Would Annie Porter please meet her party at Lost and Found, located on the purser's deck."

Annie had to ask her way to the purser's deck, and when she got there, she needed directions for Lost and Found.

Ashton, the cabin steward, lifted the sign off the doorknob, knocked once, unlocked the door and walked in. He had fresh towels and sheets draped over one arm, and he sang as he went about his work. But after closing the door behind him and taking a few steps into the cabin, he halted and his eyes popped with disbelief.

"Holy shit!" he said, looking at the wires running from the laptop up into the communications system visible where the ceiling panel had been removed. He ran one hand wonderingly along the wires.

Ashton whirled about as he heard Geiger come out of the bathroom.

"I believe I had the DO NOT DISTURB card on the door," Geiger said coldly, meanwhile closing his hand around the grip of a golf club that had been leaning against a wall.

Ashton held the card up and smiled lamely as he inched backward. "No. 'Room Make Up'," he read off the side of the card opposite DO NOT DISTURB. "Maybe you had the card flipped. Maybe I flipped the card?"

Geiger said, "Let's not split hairs."

As if that was literally what he was trying to do, he slammed the golf club down on Ashton's head.

Lost and Found was a small playroom decorated with brightly colored murals of lambs, rabbits, baby deer, and frogs, with a sprinkling of flowers. There were child-safe plastic toys scattered around on the softly carpeted floor. Alex sat on a bench next to three little kids.

One tiny girl said to him, "Your mommy will find you. Don't be afraid."

A little later, Annie knocked on the window, and his three new friends said good-bye to Alex.

Annie and Alex walked through the atrium into the shopping arcade. "I looked all over the ship twice for you," Alex said. "This place is huge."

"Good work, detective," Annie said with attitude. "You should have looked in bed, where you left me."

"You looked so beautiful, I couldn't wake you," he said. "And I ruined last night. I've never been seasick in my life."

She hesitated for a moment before saying, "What

I said after you were joking about the kids thing, for a second I thought you were serious, like you were actually asking me, you know—and last night when you were basically blacked out, I was thinking: He's a cop and I don't even know his cop number."

"What? You mean my *badge* number?"

"Badge number," she repeated. "See? Badge number—I don't even know what it's called."

"What does my badge number have to do with anything?" he asked.

"My point is, I mean, when you look at it, we barely know each other," she explained. "And getting that serious, making that kind of commitment to each other, is probably the last thing either of us wants right now, right?"

Alex felt like the wind had been taken out of his sails, but he tried to put a good face on it. "I guess so," he said.

Annie, with only a hint of disappointment, quickly changed the subject. "Ooo! Look at this," she said, stopping before a designer dress hanging in a store window. "Don't you think we were underdressed last night? Everyone's going to know me as the Woman with Two Outfits. I think it's times to ship shop," she said, getting tangled up in her words. "Can you say that ten times fast? *No.*"

Annie entered the store. Alex watched her thoughtfully for a moment before following her inside.

After sunset, Juliano, the senior officer, and Merced, the navigator, sent a message to the captain to come to the bridge. Meanwhile they went back over everything on the computers, looking for the origin of the error.

The captain walked onto the bridge and impatiently asked, "What is it?"

"I can't explain it, sir," Merced said. "We're four degrees off course."

"Switch us back to manual," the captain said, with the exaggerated patience of someone providing the simple and obvious solution.

"We've tried," Juliano told him. "Autopilot won't go down."

"Try again," the captain ordered.

.          .          .

Dressed in a ship's officer's white uniform, the jacket folded over his arm, Geiger paced on a deck area that was more out of the way, more poorly lit, and thus more deserted than other parts of the ship. He adjusted an earpiece in his right ear in order to better hear the conversation on the bridge.

"Jesus, I'm all dressed for the dance already," the captain was complaining. "What's going on?"

Geiger mumbled an answer, as if he were prompting them like characters in a play: "I sent an engineer to check the mainframe. It's all normal."

As if taking the prompt, Juliano's voice came over the earpiece: "I sent Karl to run a mainframe diagnostic. It's all fine."

Geiger smiled, pleased with his powers of prediction. "Human error," he next suggested and moved across the deck to a steel ladder. He began to climb it.

Wearing a robe, Annie was considering her two wardrobe choices for the evening when she was interrupted by a knock on the cabin door. "Is that Ashton?" she called.

"Would you prefer Ashton?" Alex called back from the other side of the door.

She went to the door and opened it. Alex stood there, in a black tuxedo, holding a gift box. Their eyes locked. Annie tried not to smile. She glanced down at his shoes. He was still wearing sneakers.

"They didn't have size tens," he explained. "I told them that's okay, size doesn't matter. But they wouldn't let me have them." He held out the gift box to her. "Now you're the Woman with Three Outfits."

Annie took the box. She thought she might be blushing.

"And one more thing," he continued.

"What?"

"I'd like to boogie with you."

Captain Pollard walked up the steep staircase that led to the ship's observation platform. When he reached the platform, he saw that an officer was already there. He assumed it was Merced—and walked over to him. A light rain had begun to fall from the starless night sky.

"We're still four degrees off course," the captain said. "Did you check the satellite, Merced?"

The man he assumed was Merced turned around to face him. It was Geiger.

"Captain Pollard, what are you doing up here?" Geiger asked in mock surprise. "How could you be running the ship if you're not on the bridge? Who's running this ship? Oh, yeah . . . I am."

Pollard was not feigning his surprise. "What is this? Who are you?"

"I spent a great many years developing computer

systems for these cruise ships, including this beauty," Geiger said, "but then I got tossed away."

"What are you talking about?"

"See?" Geiger yelled at him. "That's an example of
what infuriates me—you don't even know what I'm
talking about. That's what they all tell me!"

Geiger gave the captain a sudden push, knocking
him off balance. He used Pollard's own momentum to
throw him against the ship's rail and tip him over it.

As the captain fell, Geiger leaned over the rail
and yelled after him, "Isn't the captain supposed to
go down with the ship?"

Pollard fell straight down, more than seventy
feet, into the water alongside the ship. His body
was immediately pulled under and dragged toward
the whirling blades of the propeller.

Geiger noticed that the captain's gold-braided
cap had fallen on the platform. He picked it up and
was heading for the ladder when a woman's voice
came from the staircase.

"Captain?" the woman queried.

Geiger whirled around and came face-to-face
with the Fisher sisters, Ruby and Fran. Fran was
doing the talking.

"Would you mind if my sister had her picture
taken with you?" she asked.

Geiger looked at them both. They must have seen
nothing. They couldn't fake it if they had. They'd
both be hysterical. But it had only been a matter of
seconds. Lady luck was still on his side. Geiger let out

a long sigh of relief, and in gratitude he turned on the charm for what he saw as two slightly dotty old girls.

He put on the captain's cap—which had caused their misidentification of him, of course—and strolled over to Ruby, who was nervously tittering. He put his arm around her and smiled for the camera.

"Shoot!" he said to Fran.

She took several photos, until she and Ruby decided they'd had enough of being out in the light rain. Then they ran for shelter.

"Got a tropical storm coming in," he called after them. "The water will be beautiful tonight, ladies."

The main computer monitor at the engineers' work station in the engine room began to flash data in rapid succession. No engineers happened to be at the work station—as usual, they were performing tasks or running maintenance checkups on the engine room machinery. The program running on the computer stopped for confirmation. A question appeared on the monitor screen:

DO YOU WISH PROGRAM TO CONTINUE?
OK    CANCEL

The pause was short. Someone—not in the engine room—clicked on the OK button and the program continued. After a few minutes the question appeared again and the program was halted until confirmation was received. The OK came again without delay and the program ran its course, before abruptly disappearing and leaving a blank screen.

On engine 3A, the oil lube pump valves automatically switched to the off position.

And in Geiger's cabin the laptop screen displayed a digital countdown in progress: 10:00 . . . 9:59 . . . 9:58 . . .


In the ballroom, scores of couples danced, while others sipped champagne and talked or listened to the band. Most of the men wore tuxes. The women wore a wide array of styles, from ankle length to mini, from see-through to vinyl, in jet-black or snow-white or a rainbow of colors. The female bandleader started out with golden oldies early in the evening and had moved on to disco by now. With this crowd, she expected to close the night with house music.

Annie and Alex were dancing. She wore a strapless black dress in a form-fitting stretch faille of polyester and Lycra. At last, she thought, at long last, they were having what they'd come for—they were having fun. In her view, this cruise was suddenly great.

Drew's parents, Celeste and Rupert, were dancing near them, in an old-fashioned, very proper manner. Annie glanced their way when they suddenly stopped dancing and just stood still on the floor. They were looking at their daughter, about fourteen years old, who was standing at the edge of the dance floor, wearing a long, light jacket. For one terrible moment Annie wondered if she was wearing anything underneath it.

Plainly the same thought had occurred to the girl's mother. Celeste signed urgently to her daughter, who pouted and looked away. Then Drew slowly and determinedly took off the jacket. She was wearing a scarlet satin slip dress that struck even Annie as daringly minimal. Her parents looked appalled.

Annie heard Rupert's agitated voice above the music as he simultaneously signed and spoke to his daughter.

"I'm sorry, honey, but that dress is not appropriate," he said, straining not to sound authoritarian or unsympathetic. "You'll have to keep the jacket on."

Drew signed back to him, shaking her head vehemently.

Annie had no idea what the girl was communicating, but Annie certainly didn't agree with the father's suggestion. If anything, wearing the jacket only made things worse.

Celeste signed and spoke to her daughter: "Do you really want the captain to see you half naked?"

"Drew, I want you to go downstairs, and get changed, right now," her father signed and said with newfound firmness.

Drew glanced at Annie and Alex, but they avoided her eyes and continued dancing. She then stormed past her parents and flounced out the double doors of the ballroom in her red slip dress, trailing the jacket from one hand along the floor behind her.

Her parents followed her with their eyes. They saw her stop at the bank of elevators opposite the ballroom entrance and press the DOWN button.

Rupert placed his hand on Celeste's arm. "It's okay. Let her go," he said. "She'll be back."

They were still watching when an elevator arrived and its doors slid open. Drew stepped inside. Before the doors could close behind her, she tossed her jacket out.


Engine 3A was making grinding noises and vibrating more than normal. The grinding and shaking were growing progressively stronger. Lights flashed on monitor screens and an electronic warning beep sounded throughout the ship's engine room.

"Jesus Christ! The V pumps are off!" an engineer shouted.

Another engineer spoke urgently into a radio transmitter, watching black smoke rise in slow coils from the engine.

Juliano and Merced were being alerted on the bridge by engine room monitor screens, which were flashing so many red lights they were like Christmas decorations.

"What the hell is going on?" Juliano asked, without expecting an answer.

"I don't know, sir," Merced responded politely.

"Where's the chief engineer?" Juliano asked, again not requiring a response, and this time not getting one.

In his cabin, Geiger put on the captain's gold-braid cap and looked at himself in the mirror. He smiled in approval of what he saw. He then looked across at the laptop screen. The countdown was progressing: 4:13 . . . 4:12 . . .

Annie and Alex danced slow and close, as the female bandleader sang a torrid song. They glided around, lost in their own private world, not noticing Celeste and Rupert sitting watchfully, waiting for their daughter to return. Nor did they notice Debbie and Harvey, who had just about mugged a waiter for his tray of food and were now splitting the take.

As they danced, Alex began to talk softly to Annie. There was a sincerity in his tone that made her pay close attention to his words. "I left you this morning because I needed to think," he said. "Yeah, my job may be dangerous. But what gets me through it, the one thing I can trust, is my instinct. Which has never been more certain about anything than it is about us." They twirled among multi-colored spotlights. "There's nothing in the world I'm ever going to want more than this," he said.

"Really?" Annie asked. She gazed deeply into his eyes, feeling swept away.

At the engineers' work station, the chief engineer and two colleagues scanned the screens and digital displays. The chief engineer shook his head and rapped out an order: "Shut down numbers three and four! And get everybody out of there!"

Obeying his order, crew members closed valves and pushed buttons and levers on the huge, quivering engines. The men worked fast and methodically, looking out for each other. Then they all left the danger area of the engine room in a hurry, doing a fast roll call of names as they left, to make sure they were leaving no one behind.

In the ballroom Annie and Alex were still dancing and talking earnestly.

"So?" she asked. "What are you saying?"

"I'm saying that we—"

BOOM! The whole ship shuddered. Dancers stumbled, drinks spilled, the band stopped playing. Passengers looked at one another worriedly.

In a panic, Annie called out, "No, no, not now!"

"We gotta get out of here," Alex said.

Even the bridge was shaking. Watching the digital displays from the engine room, Juliano said urgently into a telephone, "They're not going to hold! Close the fuel valves!" He said to the others on the bridge, "Somebody get the captain!"

While he was saying this, Geiger was leaning

back in his cabin, watching the countdown on his laptop screen: 2:34 . . . 2:33 . . .

He cheerfully shook in his chair along with the quaking ship. "Took less time than I thought," he commented aloud, amused at how he'd underestimated his powers. Looking over at the jar of slowly twisting leeches, he said fondly to them, "Hang on, you little vampires! We're gonna shake, rattle, 'n' roll!"


The shuddering that racked the entire ship persisted much longer than passengers could regard as normal, and many were becoming panicky. No explanation had been offered by the captain on the public address system—and, of course, if the passengers had known that the captain was no longer on board, it would not have helped any.

Champagne slopped from glasses, glassware slid from tables and shattered on the polished floor, food fell and adhered to evening gowns and carpets. Pictures dropped off the walls. The band started to play again, like bands are supposed to during disasters, in order to calm the crowd. When they heard the band start up once more, some people who hadn't worried till then decided that it was an eerie sound and drifted—they tried not to rush—toward the exit.

"Oh, Frank," Constance said to her husband, "it's an earthquake!"

Annie heard this and remembered her earthquake drill. "Get under the tables!" she shouted.

"This isn't an earthquake," Alex protested.

"It's close enough!" Annie insisted.


In his easy chair, Geiger watched unconcerned as his prescription bottles rattled on a shelf and toppled, one by one, to the cabin floor. But when the jar of leeches started sliding along the top of a chest of drawers and seemed headed for a similar fate, he quickly rose and saved it. He returned to the easy chair, cradling the leech jar on his lap. Then he went back to watching the laptop screen intently.

The digital countdown was ending: 0:02 . . . 0:01 . . .

Geiger closed his eyes and waited.


The needles on all the engine dials moved into the red zone, and hooters sounded the alert on all engine room levels. The chief engineer had personally checked that all fire doors leading to the danger area had been sealed. He'd done all he could do. Circumstances were now outside his control.

The chief engineer was thinking these thoughts when he was lifted a foot off his chair by the shock of a nearby blast.

The tempered steel back of engine 3A lifted off. The impact wave of air was powerful enough in itself to knock down the wall between the engine room and the engineers' work station.

Elsewhere, engine parts whistled like artillery shells and destroyed what they hit. None of the engineers or crew were hurt. They were all left standing in the work station, with a clear view into the engine room where the wall used to be.

The exploding engine caused the entire ship to heel to one side in the water. This was the final straw for most passengers. One side of the ballroom floor lifted up until the entire room was at an angle. Chairs, tables, anything not bolted to the floor moved in ghostly fashion from the high side of the ballroom to the lower. Many of the people found themselves sliding downhill along with the furniture.

Everyone got a sinking feeling in their stomachs as the ship heeled over to its full extent . . . then began the big slide back as the ship righted itself and began to lean in the other direction. All the tables and chairs began to move back to where they'd been.

Chandeliers fell from the ceiling, and the crystals scattered beneath people's feet. Many passengers had given up all pretense at calm—they ran for their lives to the exit doors, pushing and shoving those who got in their way.

Annie looked at Alex. "Please, this is my vacation," she pleaded. "I just want to relax . . . at least once."

Alex pointed to himself. "I had nothing to do with this!"

People were screaming. One passenger yelled, "We've hit an iceberg!"

Geiger kept his eyes shut and clutched the jar of leeches through the engine explosion and the rocking of the ship that followed. When the motion subsided somewhat, he opened his eyes and gave himself a satisfied smile in the mirror. Rising from the easy chair, he replaced the leech jar on the chest of drawers and went to the laptop. He rapidly keyboarded in data and set a new program running. A graphical depiction of the ship's bridge formed on the screen.

Throughout the ship, surges and failures in the power systems knocked out some operations and left others nearby untouched. In the vault room, power changes set off an alarm system that automatically swung the heavy vault door closed and caused the locking device to move on its lubricated bearings. The merchandise of the Diamond Jewelers of America was now safe from potential looters who might take advantage of the widespread panic on the ship.

Drew was less fortunate with the elevator power system. The elevator she'd gotten into after her parents ordered her to change her dress had stopped at the floor beneath, and it took forever for about nine drunk adults to get on. As soon as they realized that the elevator was going down, instead of up to the ballroom, one of them pressed the button to open the doors, and so the doors opened again.

This led to further discussion, especially with one sloshed individual who was convinced they were misinformed and that the direction in which the elevator would travel was up—he indicated this direction with his forefinger—not down. A few of the party were undecided. In fact, some of them didn't even seem to know they were on an elevator.

Someone else suggested leaving the decision to Drew. But one idiot, who she guessed had seen her signing earlier in the day, did a lot of whispering and gesticulating in her direction. Drew didn't even bother to read their lips. Some of them looked at her and smiled, kind of embarrassed. Then they pushed the others out of the elevator ahead of them, including the argumentative man who was still saying he was convinced that the elevator was, contrary to their expectations, about to travel upward.

Drew was alone again. She felt like she'd spent an hour with them as the doors finally closed and the elevator eased gently downward. At least they hadn't complained about her dress!

Suddenly the elevator stopped, just like that, between floors. Drew couldn't believe it. She pushed buttons for lower floors, then those for upper floors. Nothing happened. She saw the red emergency button, but didn't press it, not wanting to be Little Miss Panic-Stricken, just because an elevator stopped between floors.

Then the elevator lights went out.

She was all alone now, in total silence—which she was used to—and total darkness. Since she couldn't hear, she knew that she might be missing all kinds of information. Not being able to see, not being able to take in visible information, cut her off completely from the world. But she was not going to panic, yet. All the same, she leaned hard on the emergency button and hoped that by now a loud ringing sound was alerting everyone that one of the elevators was stuck. It would serve her parents right if something happened to her. They should have let her wear her pretty red dress which she'd bought on her own with money she had earned herself. Instead, they had sent her back to change. They'd never forgive themselves. . . .

Then the elevator began to shake violently from side to side, and she screamed.

On the bridge, the computer screens and digital displays were still flitting like lights in Las Vegas. A large pot of coffee had hit the floor tiles, and the brown liquid swilled back and forth with the ship's motion. None of the ship's officers paid any attention—they had more important things on their minds. Juliano and Merced were sending instruction over phones, checking details with one another as they did so.

"Auxiliary malfunction!" one officer called out, pointing to the screen with the relevant data. Then he quickly pointed to another screen. "Structural trauma! Take a look at the monitors!"

"We're losing power all over the ship," Merced said, putting down his phone. "Where the hell is Engine Control?"

"I want all emergency teams in position," Juliano ordered. "Get the Coast Guard on the line."

At that moment, in the ship's communications room, a small explosion scattered the wiring everywhere like loose straw.

One officer on the bridge looked at the phone receiver in his hand. "It's dead," he said. "What's happened?"

"Try the low frequencies," Juliano said.

Merced was already trying those. "The signal is gone," he said. "We got nothing."

• • •

The shaking had stopped in the ballroom. The furniture was no longer moving about on its own, and things had stopped falling off the ceiling and walls. But the panic had not subsided.

Liza, the entertainment director, was trying to exert the magic of her personality. The more she tried to reassure people, the more convinced they became that they were in some kind of trouble.

"I'm sure this is only a drill," she said over the microphone on the bandstand. The musicians had all disappeared by then. With a weak smile, she waved at people to attract their attention to what she was saying. "We'll have everything back to normal in a few minutes."

Most of the people in the ballroom had gone. Those left behind were mostly the kind of people left behind in any disaster—those slowed by physical or mental or emotional infirmities or by a sense of duty to those less fortunate than themselves.

Alex belonged firmly in the public servant category. Annie couldn't help feeling that he'd conned her in some way. Here they were on a cruise to paradise—three thousand miles from the bullets and bloodletting of the LAPD SWAT team—in a gleaming white ship on a baby blue sea—except that it was nighttime, though at least they were beneath tropical skies—and what did she get? This! Alex going around in his best law enforcement officer way, helping people to their feet, checking them for injuries and asking her to calm them down while he went on to rescue someone else lying on the ballroom floor.

"I'm sure this is only a drill," Liza shouted above the din. "Everything should be back to normal in a few moments."

"How come I don't really believe her?" Annie asked.

Alex shrugged and said, "So far tonight's pretty romantic, don't you think?"

Two more ship's officers rushed onto the bridge. They saw that the place was in chaos and that nothing was working.

"What can I do, sir?" one asked.

"Try to run a link to the engine room," Juliano instructed him. "And issue handheld radios to all the crew. And somebody find the captain!"

A bridge radio unit beeped twice.

Juliano pressed the speaker phone button and said, "Yes?"

"Mr. Juliano, it looks like the *Seabourn Legend* isn't faring too well," a man's voice said. "I advise you to begin the evacuation procedure."

"Who is this?" Juliano asked. He gestured to the other officers to stop what they were doing and to listen in on this strange conversation.

"This is someone you should start listening to,"

Geiger said. "I want you to sound the evacuation alarm immediately. Time is running out."

"I can't order an evacuation," Juliano snapped. "The captain is the only one authorized—"

"The captain is dead, Mr. Juliano, which means you are now responsible for the people on this ship."

All the ship's officers were stunned by this news.

Geiger's voice continued over the bridge address system, "Don't waste time trying to call the Coast Guard or code in an SOS—I've cut off all outside communications."

"Wait!" Juliano said urgently. "You don't understand . . . I can't! Maritime regulations state that—"

"Mr. Juliano, you are in command of this vessel," Geiger's voice interrupted. "The authority is yours! But I'll make it easier for you." There was a pause during which they could hear keyboarding sounds over the speaker phone. Then the voice returned: "I'd like you to look at the emergency fire display."

Juliano and Merced walked quickly to that monitor screen.

The voice continued, "Look at the port side of B deck, section 212 on your display."

"What do you think you're doing?" Juliano asked, playing for time.

Unseen by the officers on the bridge, a golf ball smoke grenade exploded behind the grill of an air-conditioning vent in a corridor on the left side of B deck. The blast was small and caused no physical damage, but the vast quantity of thick white smoke that resulted was out of all proportion to its incendiary source. The incoming air from the vent blew the smoke into the corridor. Smoke detectors responded.

Section 212 lighted up on the bridge emergency fire display.

"Oops!" Geiger's voice said playfully over the speaker phone. "See what you made me do?"

"Okay!" Juliano pleaded desperately. "Wait a minute! Wait a minute!"

"And now the forward section of the crew deck, on both sides of the bow thrusters," the voice continued, on the verge of crazy laughter. He elaborated: "Sections 111, 341, 535, 299 . . ."

On the crew deck, golf ball smoke grenades were exploding all over and the corridors were filling with heavy foglike smoke.

Corresponding lights began blinking on the bridge emergency fire display—a lot of lights. As the smoke spread to other areas, fire alarms went off and new lights signaled on the display. Printers rattled and paper streams of fire alarm records moved steadily into collection boxes. To the officers on the bridge, it felt like they were standing on a woodpile and someone was dropping lighted matches into it.

Juliano looked wildly around him and imagined he smelled smoke. "My God . . ." was all he could think of to say.

The voice came back over the speaker phone, now filled with gloating menace: "All of these fires are contained by fire doors, which I control—and will open if necessary. I have charges positioned throughout the ship—and will set them off without hesitation."

Merced looked meaningfully at the ship's evacuation alarm button and said to Juliano, forgetting to lower his voice so as not to be heard over the speaker phone: "Sir, I think you should push the evacuation button."

Juliano looked despairingly at the flashing lights on the emergency fire display. "It's not possible," he answered, speaking in his normal voice. "I can't abandon ship while it's moving."

The voice on the speaker phone now came through in a tone of cold command: "The ship will be stopped in exactly three minutes. I'll give you fifteen minutes to evacuate. Now, sound the alarm . . . or I'll burn her down."

Juliano looked first at Merced and then at the evacuation alarm button.

"Sir, I really think you should press the button," Merced said with quiet intensity.

Alex and Annie were still clearing people from the ballroom, and helping those who were still in shock, when they heard seven short, ear-splitting toots followed by a long one.

Juliano's voice came over the ship's public address system: "All passengers and crew proceed to the muster deck. This is not a drill. The *Seabourn Legend* is to be immediately evacuated."

Annie looked at Alex in total outrage. This really was too much.

He didn't like the way she kept looking at him, as if he had something to do with all this stuff that was happening. He just shrugged.

Juliano's voice came back over the speakers: "This is not a drill. Please remain calm." It had been a comparatively long time now since any of the passengers had felt calm. "Crew will assist passengers into lifeboats. All hands, all passengers . . . abandon ship. Do not go to your cabins. Leave all possessions, and proceed immediately to . . ."

Annie looked at Alex once more. She couldn't believe this! She had a hard time getting the words out: "Abandon ship?"

The officers and crew went through the ship, banging on cabin doors, looking into lounges, urging passengers to forget their belongings and protect their lives by going without delay to the muster deck. Alarms were ringing and announcements were repeated over the ship's public address system.

People gathered under floodlights on the muster deck. They looked fearfully out at the pitch-dark waters. The seas were calm, but there was no sign of any lights out there, signifying land or other ships. It was dark and empty. Lifeboats filled with passengers were being lowered to the water, each hitting the surface with a slapping sound and a big splash. Crew members were inflating rubber rafts from metal drums on the decks and dropping the rafts over the side. Others were dropping rope ladders from various decks down the sides of the ship to reach the water. Officers assured passengers there would be room for everyone in the lifeboats, and that the ropes and ladders were just added precautionary measures.

Debbie and Harvey hurried down a long corridor. They came upon a dozen or so people at a closed fire door. The group included Liza, the sisters Fran and Ruby, the newlyweds Isabel and Alejandro, and Constance and Frank, the dignified couple who sat at the next table to them in the dining room—back when it looked like they all might have an enjoyable cruise.

"What's the problem?" Sheri Silver, the woman bandleader asked, lacking her usual star-quality self-assurance. She added plaintively, "I have to get out."

"This door won't open," Alejandro said, his macho image still more or less intact.

"I know a shortcut," Liza piped up, full of ideas, as always. "Everyone take a hand—grab a safety buddy."

"Shut up, Liza," Sheri said, getting some of her sparkle back. "Just show us!"

They followed Liza down another corridor and turned a corner. About twenty feet ahead of them they saw another fire door very slowly swinging closed. Frank ran toward it.

"Get your hand in there!" Constance called after him.

Frank made it in time and was about to stick his hand into the narrowing space between the metal door and the door frame when he thought better of it. The fire door closed firmly, and Frank could not open it when he tried. The group was now isolated between several fire doors, all closed and unopenable.

"Oh, God!" Debbie gasped. "We're trapped!"

"I need a cigarette, Frank," Constance said in a tremulous voice. "I really need a cigarette."


Thin layers of smoke hung in the air as Annie and Alex moved with other passengers toward the muster deck.

"Alex, this can't happen," Annie maintained. "The brochure said they have a thousand sprinklers and this special gas they can release if a fire—"

Alex stopped in his tracks, struck by what she had just said. He sniffed the air. "Sulfur," he said. "Do you smell that? It's sulfur."

Annie could almost see his thought processes spinning. "So?" she prodded.

He started to head down another corridor, away from the passengers bound for the muster deck. "I want to check this out," he said. "Just a quick detour. I think something's wrong—"

"Yeah, there is!" Annie cut in. "We're abandoning ship in the middle of the night! Alex, come on . . ."

"I promise I'll be right back, Annie," he said. "Follow the crew. I won't be long."

Standing alone in the totally dark steel box, stuck between floors, Drew searched with her hands and pressed every button she found several times. The red emergency button stood out in her memory as being bigger than the other buttons. She'd found it, and by now had pressed it at least twenty times.

Drew had recovered from her panic once the elevator had stopped shaking so violently. While that was going on, she'd expected to drop like a stone to the bottom of the shaft at any second. She was in control again now, for the time being, at least—she felt panic flickering like flames in brushwood somewhere in the back of her mind. But she was no chicken. That was one thing about her handicap: being deaf had thrown her back on her own resources at an early age. She often felt she was stronger inside than most people. She had no choice, of course. She had to be.

Not being claustrophobic or afraid of the dark, she could devote her thoughts to logical, practical things, like finding a way to get out of there. But her thinking was limited to what she knew. She was in an elevator that was out of order. Sooner or later, people had to notice it or hear the alarm bell ringing. It never occurred to her that the problem extended beyond her elevator and that her one alarm was lost among the many others that were sounding.

She continued to methodically use her hands to feel around inside the elevator in the dark, thinking with grim humor that this was like being deaf *and* blind, trying to throw the cold water of reason on those little flames of panic flickering in the back of her mind.

All this because of her stupid parents and her stupid red dress!


Celeste and Rupert refused to be herded toward the lifeboats.

"We can't find our daughter," Rupert explained to a young ship's officer. "She wasn't in the cabin. It's room 8127."

"That's B deck—it's already evacuated," the officer responded. "There's nothing to worry about—"

"But she's deaf," Celeste explained. "Isn't there some way we can—"

"Folks, we've got her," the officer assured them. "I cleared that deck myself. She's in good hands. Now you're going to have to get up to the muster deck if you want to catch up to her."

The officer ushered them along the corridor toward the doors leading to the muster deck. He urged them past a bank of elevators. Over one elevator door a red light was blinking. All the fire alarms sounding together were deafening.

. . .

Merced was alone on the bridge, still trying to free the ship's steering from the autopilot. He knew it was beyond his ability, but persisted intently keyboarding instructions into the computer. They were ignored or rejected. He made new changes and tried again. Then he suddenly seemed to be making progress—until the computer stopped accepting the input.

"Christ!" he said in frustration. "He's shut us out!"

At that moment the door was thrown open behind him. Merced cringed. "Don't kill me!" he pleaded. He peered back over his shoulder, saw it was Alex and said in relief, "Get to the lifeboats, sir! You'll only get in the way up here!"

"Take it easy, I'm LAPD," Alex assured him, without it occurring to him that Merced might not know what the initials represented. "I just want to check something."

"You're what?" Merced asked.

It took only a few seconds for Alex to scan the emergency fire display, with its numerous flashing alarm lights. "Have any of the fires been confirmed?" he asked.

"We're loading the lifeboats!" Merced said. "You need more confirmation than that?"

Looking through the bridge windows, they could see the small navigation lights of some of the lifeboats that had already pulled away from the nearly stationary cruise ship.

Below them, deep in the ship, in the only cabin still occupied, Geiger tested a half-full bathtub of water to make sure it was no more than tepid. Satisfied that it was not too hot or too cold, he emptied the leeches into it. He looked down fondly at them swimming around in their twitching way and said aloud to them, "Sorry I can't take you all with me. But you can make a swim for it soon."

Under the floodlights on muster deck, the ship's photographer took shots of the lifeboats being lowered.

"Lower number seven!" Juliano ordered.

Electric winches lowered the lifeboat filled with passengers over the side of the ship and kept a steady pace until, a minute later, the boat hit the sea with a slap and a splash. The occupants disconnected the winch cables from the prow and stern of the lifeboat, started the engine and were away.

"Let's move!" Juliano called. "Last boat, everybody goes right now!"

The last of the passengers climbed into the lifeboat, except for Annie. Come hell or high water, she was waiting for Alex. And Drew's parents, who looked worried sick.

"Annie," Celeste said, clinging to her, "Drew wasn't in the room."

"We searched everywhere," Rupert said.

"We can't leave without her!" Celeste wailed.

Annie was still watching for some sign of Alex. She said, "She must be in another lifeboat."

"Come on, let's go!" Juliano urged the three of them.

To her intense relief, Annie saw Alex running toward them. "Alex!" she called. "Come on, this is the last boat!"

Celeste turned to Alex. "Did you find Drew?" she asked.

Alex didn't answer but instead questioned Juliano: "Didn't you run a count?"

"Sir, you're gonna have to get into that boat!" Juliano insisted. "I'm responsible for the passengers on this ship!"

"Your board is lighting up from flash grenades and sulfur-based smoke canisters," Alex informed him. "Half those fires don't exist. So what the hell's going on?"

Juliano rapidly explained what he knew, which wasn't a whole lot. Only two things he said really mattered. First, this catastrophe was not due to a series of mechanical failures and unfortunate coincidences—there was a madman on board making these things happen. The second thing was that they were working against time—they had been given fifteen minutes to evacuate the ship.

"There's no time left!" Juliano said, glancing at his watch. "I don't know what this guy is capable of. We have to get this boat off!"

. . .

Carrying empty bags, Geiger left his cabin and walked through deserted corridors. When he arrived at the vault room, he pointed his handheld computer at the massive vault door. His index finger keyboarded in a series of commands, which were answered by a whirring of the lock mechanism. The heavy door opened automatically on its hinges. Geiger had known that the vault had its own power system, independent of the ship's.

He looked inside and saw light beams crisscrossing. Breaking a single one of them would set off multiple alarms, which would only raise the decibel level a little of all the alarms presently going off. He knew there were also invisible infrared rays that did the same thing, plus heat and movement sensors. But all they did was make noise and set off flashing lights on distant consoles. None of that mattered anymore. He walked in and set off the alarms.

The shelves of the vault contained the locked jewel boxes of the Diamond Jewelers of America. Inside were all those stones that models had been dazzling people with, displayed on black velvet. They were now his for the taking.

A shrill beep on his handheld computer brought Geiger's attention to its miniature screen. He read the words: EVAC PROGRAM COMPLETED. He had given them fifteen minutes, and that was all they would get. If the dull-witted bastards hadn't gotten their lard asses off the ship by now, they could suffer the consequences. His forefinger pressed the enter key and the screen went blank momentarily before the following appeared: STENA CONVOY PROGRAM START UP CONFIRM. He keyboarded in the code response. The screen blinked and countered: ARE YOU SURE? Again, he keyboarded the coded response. The words faded as the program ran. After a few seconds the screen flashed the words: THANK YOU, CAPTAIN. PROGRAM LOCKED AND SECURED.

Far beneath him, in the ship's deserted engine room, the big diesel engines roared back to life.

Geiger felt the vibrations of the ship's engines in the vault. "We're on our way," he said triumphantly.

On the muster deck, Drew's parents were at last persuaded by Juliano to get into the lifeboat. Alex begged Annie to get in. She was holding onto him tight as she stepped into the boat, in order to try to bring him in along with her. The lifeboat swayed gently on its winch cables as it dangled over the side of the ship, high above the darkness. They could hear but not see the water far beneath.

As Annie was about to step in, the ship lurched forward and the lifeboat went into a free fall toward the water. Annie was left stepping into empty air over the side of the ship. Alex gripped her tightly and held on. For a moment it was touch and go, as they teetered at a gap in the deck rail where the lifeboat had been. Juliano grabbed Alex's arm and together they hauled her back on deck. Annie looked Alex in the eyes. She knew now that he would do that for her—fall overboard in an effort to save her. But an instant later this wonderful feeling was spoiled for her by the realization that Alex, with his SWAT team mindset, would probably have done the same for anyone, even his worst enemy. He'd done nothing special for her!

The lifeboat fell about halfway to the water level. The passengers clung to one another and to the boat's sides, all managing to stay inside the craft.

Alex ran to the officer holding the remote control device for the winches. "Bring them up!" he said.

"I'm trying," the officer said. "It's not working."

The ship was now under way once more and picking up speed. Leaning over the side, the people on the muster deck could hear the shouts and screams of those in the lifeboat and, through the darkness, see that it had begun to swing on the cables and bang against the white side of the ship. The faster the ship went, the more the lifeboat swung on the cables and the harder it slammed into the hull. And the louder the people in the lifeboat yelled for help.

Celeste looked at the thin cables supporting the boat she was in. "They're gonna break!" she screamed.

"Bring us up!" a lifeboat crew member hollered to those above.

"I can't!" the ship's officer yelled down. "The winch is jammed."

While the passengers in the lifeboat were in the seats they'd been assigned, the boat was balanced. But those on the ship side of the lifeboat now moved away from where the boat was slamming against the steel hull, which caused the boat to tip sideways toward the ocean, almost sending several passengers into the water. They clung to whatever they could and screamed and struck out at the others, who saw no reason why they themselves should be crushed to death against the ship's side. From their continuing movements and struggles, the boat rocked from side to side, banging into the side of the ship.

Looking down over the rail into the darkness, Alex could see it would only be a matter of time before most of the lifeboat's occupants were pitched into the sea beside the already fast-moving ship. And once in the water, they would be drawn beneath the ship's underside.

"You have to stop the ship," Alex said to Juliano.

"I don't have any control," the senior officer replied.

"The cables aren't going to hold," Alex said. "We have to get them out of there."

"Stay out of our way!" Juliano snapped, resentful that this passenger was telling him what needed doing.

Alex paid him no heed. He had more important things on his mind—like getting down there to those people in the lifeboat before they brought down even more serious trouble upon themselves. A short way along the deck, he found a rope ladder hanging over the side, secured to the deck rail. He untied it and, without drawing the ladder up, moved it until it hung close to the lifeboat. He then retied it to the rail.

Juliano, other officers, and the crew were too busy trying to fix the winches to notice what he was doing—until he climbed over the rail and started down the rope ladder on the side of the ship.

Juliano ran over to the rail and stared down in horror. "What the hell is he doing?" he asked, aghast.

"He said he'd be right back," Annie said casually, as if Alex had gone to the store for a six-pack.


Passengers in the lifeboat clutched at the end of the rope ladder.

"Don't move around!" Alex warned them as he moved down the rungs as fast as he could.

"They have to pull us up!" one male passenger shouted, an edge of hysteria in his voice.

"Stay calm," Alex advised. "Keep the weight balanced. I'm gonna bring you up one at a time."

What he said to them about staying calm would have been more convincing if the rope ladder hadn't begun swaying off the side of the fast-moving ship, just like the lifeboat was doing, and smashing Alex against the hull. The first two times, he was able to keep at arm's length from the ship's steel plates, because he wasn't that far down the ladder and did not hit the side with much force. But once he got down the ladder a good way, he felt himself swinging away from the ship's side and out over the dark void above open water. As he began to swing back again, he saw the side of the ship coming and held tight, relaxing his body and trying to roll with the impact. But this was a head-on impact with a huge surface— there was nowhere to roll to avoid the full force of collision. Rather than hit him a glancing blow, the ship seemed to want to squash him like a fly.

The force of the impact knocked his feet off the ladder and left him hanging by his hands, with his knuckles scraping along the ship's side. The smoothly painted surface of the new ship did not skin his knuckles, but the blow almost winded him. Alex knew he had to reach the lifeboat before the next swing-out-and-back cycle occurred.

He got his feet back on the ladder rungs and started clambering down as fast as he could. He was only a few feet above the lifeboat when Celeste lost control. She jumped up from her seat in the boat and tried to run toward the rope ladder.

"She's still there!" she screamed. "I know Drew's still on the ship!"

"Celeste, what are you doing?" Rupert said, desperately trying to catch her. "Come back!"

Alex saw something happening to one of the

cables. "Don't move!" he shouted down to Celeste. "This cable can break!"

She was not going to be stopped. On her way to the bow, she clambered over seats and other passengers, avoiding restraining hands and causing the boat rock every which way. Clawing her way to the rope ladder, she tried to pull Alex off it so she could climb up. Other passengers, disturbed by her, were shifting around at the bow end of the boat too, paying no heed to Alex's warnings as the winch cable curled in on itself.

In a split second the cable slipped six feet or more, tipping the bow end of the lifeboat downward. Alex grabbed Celeste, and they were left hanging together on the rope ladder. Passengers in the boat grabbed and held onto whatever they could. But two passengers who'd been on their feet in the bow—a woman and a man—were thrown overboard. They disappeared into the darkness below, their screams getting fainter as they fell the equivalent of four stories, to be lost forever in the nighttime, shark-infested Caribbean.

Witnessing these two deaths quieted everybody down more powerfully than any reasonable entreaties had been able to. The other passengers just looked accusingly at Celeste as Alex helped her down the ladder and into the lifeboat. She at least had shut up and was doing what she was told. Also, everybody in the boat now had enough to occupy their minds, what with the boat tipping downward at the bow and seaward along the side, meanwhile swinging on its cables and banging against the side of the ship. No amusement park had come up with a ride like this!

Alex had no idea what made the cable slip or why it had only slipped so far and no more. He stayed on the ladder and examined the steel strands. They were badly frayed all along the length he could see. He looked up at the dim faces at the deck rail far above him and made out Annie and Juliano.

"This cable won't hold," he said, trying to keep his voice calm. The last thing he needed was to have people jumping around in panic in the lifeboat again. That would tip them all into the sea. "I need another cable." He tried to make it sound like asking for another cup of coffee.

Juliano signaled that he could get one and went with crew members to fetch it. Annie stayed at the deck rail, looking down at Alex on the rope ladder, which was now swinging outward over the sea before coming in to bang against the swiftly moving ship's side once more. As they swung inward, Alex, on the rope ladder, now on the same level as the lifeboat, became positioned between the boat and the side of the ship. When the boat hit the ship, he would be crushed between them. Annie could see he was looking the other way and hadn't seen the danger he was in.

"Alex!" she screamed as loud as her lungs would let her.

He heard the warning in her voice, tensed and looked for danger. He saw it coming only just in time—and kicked off the bow of the in-swinging boat like a mountain rappeler. The heavy boat, traveling faster than he was, passed him and banged against the steel plates. The boat's gunwale would have cut him in two. He looked up and gave Annie a V sign. And then whacked against the side of the ship himself.

Neither he nor the lifeboat were going to be able to take much more of this. By this time, however, crew members on the muster deck had lowered a steel cable down into the swaying lifeboat.

"Grab the line!" Alex shouted to them.

Wrong thing to say! Several of the passengers, getting to their feet to move after it, nearly tipped the boat over. One man grabbed the cable and held on tightly. Alex recognized him instantly as the ship's photographer, who had endlessly tried to peddle portraits to him and Annie and who they later learned was rather improbably named Dante, presumably after the great Italian poet. All looked well for a moment. But then the movement of the lifeboat caused Dante to loose his footing. Fortunately for him, he kept a tight hold on the cable. The lifeboat tilted oceanward. Dante went over the side—or at least the lower half of him did. His head and shoulders were still in the boat as he clutched the cable.

"Alex, he's gonna fall!" Annie yelled down.

Alex had independently come to a fairly similar conclusion. He didn't hesitate. He jumped off the rope ladder and landed hard in the lifeboat.

"Oh, God!" Annie called out. She hadn't meant for Alex to do that.

Crawling along the lifeboat floor, Alex tried to keep the boat balanced. He grabbed Dante by the wrists and held him suspended above the ocean far below. It required all his strength.

"Hold on!" Alex ground out, more to himself than to Dante.

Some passengers moved to help, causing the lifeboat to tilt even more.

"We're all gonna fall!" someone yelled.

"Nobody move!" Alex said in his best LAPD manner.

Then, very slowly, he tried to pull Dante up over the side and into the boat.

Looking down, Annie could see that this was causing the boat to slowly tip over sideways. She frantically looked for something that might help. She noticed the metal gangplank secured to the side of the ship at a level beneath the lifeboat. Up till then, she hadn't seen it in the darkness. If the lifeboat couldn't be winched up, perhaps they could lower it. Annie tried to explain this to the senior officer.

Juliano was securing the cable. "Help her!" he told the other officers.

After a few words from her, they ran to extend the forty-foot gangplank out the side of the ship. Alex managed to drag Dante into the boat—and then nearly ended up in the sea anyway as the boat's occupants peered over the side to see the gangplank being extended beneath them. Alex steadied them down and made them stay in place while he secured the steel cable to the bow in place of the frayed one. When it was secure, he gave the signal for the crew members on the muster deck to lower the lifeboat slowly onto the gangplank.

"One at a time!" Alex had to yell as the boat's occupants hurried to the comparative safety of the ship.

The elevator in which Drew was trapped had a metal handrail about four feet off the ground. But the elevator walls were otherwise smooth, and every time she tried to climb up on the handrail, she couldn't find any finger holds and fell back. Normally impatient and petulant when she didn't get her own way, alone in the dark Drew became a new person. She patiently tried to climb up over and over again, with no foot-stamping or cussing when she fell back. With no great plan in mind if she did manage to get up on the handrail, it was more important to her to keep her mind and body occupied than thinking fearfully about her predicament.

First getting one knee on the handrail, she used the pressure of her hands against the two walls in a back corner to keep herself upright as she got her second knee on the handrail. Now her problem was to get to her feet without falling backward onto the elevator floor. Pressing in opposite directions with her hands, she slowly got to one foot and then to the other, standing at last on the handrail—and managed to get one hand on the elevator ceiling to prevent herself from falling.

The ceiling was only inches above her head. Making sure her heels were firmly placed on the handrail, she felt around in the ceiling for a trapdoor. This was always how people in movies and TV shows escaped from elevators. Drew had no thought of doing anything in an elevator shaft—the idea was enough to make her tremble. She just wanted relief from being sealed in this steel box. Opening the trapdoor that she guessed was in the ceiling somewhere would open a window out onto the world, even if it was only the interior of an elevator shaft.

Her fingers found a rectangle, roughly three by two feet, in the ceiling nearby. When she pressed against it, it yielded. At last, she felt, she was having a bit of luck. If the trapdoor had been in the center of the ceiling, she could never have reached it, and it was only a matter of good fortune that it was located on the side of the elevator she managed to climb up rather than the other. Pushing upward and sideways, she moved the trapdoor aside. Before she saw anything, she felt the draft of cold salt-laden air, which was sweeter to her that moment than the scent of wildflowers.

Looking up into the elevator shaft, Drew could see light at its glassed-in top. There were also rectangles of light around closed elevator doors at various levels. She was a bit surprised to see no sign of the other elevators going up and down. She had expected that. But they all seemed to be beneath her level. Perhaps they were all out of order, which would explain why it was taking so long for someone to come rescue her. It still did not occur to her trouble existed beyond this bank of elevators. Had she known that all the passengers had already abandoned ship, except for one lifeboat load, she would have gone out of her mind.

She couldn't stay balanced on the handrail for much longer, and yet she was understandably reluctant to drop back into her steel-box prison once more, now that she'd opened a door to the exterior. Drew had an idea. She would try to pull herself up onto the roof of the elevator. When they came to rescue her, they would find her sitting in the open trapdoor on top of the elevator, instead of being a helpless female imprisoned inside it. That appealed to her.

Getting up there would require one major effort that would either succeed or wouldn't—and she'd be on her back on the elevator floor once more. It was worth trying. She placed a hand on each side of the opening and sunk down on bended knees as far as she could. Then she straightened her body fast and jumped upward. Her momentum took her high enough up inside the trapdoor to lean on her elbows and forearms. But she was still inside the elevator from the waist down, and she wasn't sure she had enough strength to push her way onto the roof. If she'd thought about it, she would have been sure that she didn't have the strength. However, there was no time for thinking. She struggled up, kicking out at the empty air beneath her. At last she got her right thigh onto the roof and then all of her body, so that she was sitting on the roof, with her legs dangling through the trapdoor. They could come rescue her now! She was ready!

She thought of her dress now, the new dress that her parents hated and which she'd paid for herself with her own money . . . It was ruined! Up here, there was all kinds of grease and oil, with dust attached. And she'd heard the fabric rip several times when she was climbing up. Why were her parents like that? Other kids had *human* parents. Hers were dinosaurs. All this was their fault, not hers.

She got to her feet and tried to see things in the shaftway. She could see the main supporting cable for each elevator high above her in the light from the top of the shaft. It was out of the question for her to try to climb up the cable supporting her elevator. What she needed to do was slide down the cable of the elevator next to her. She could see this cable down to a level about twenty feet above her head. At her level, she could sense where it ought to be, but it was too dark to see it.

With her feet, she felt for the edge of the elevator roof. She found it, only a step away from where she stood. From there, it was a sheer drop. If only she could see . . .

The elevators were small. Judging from the distance to the cable of her own elevator, the invisible cable was not more than a foot or so beyond her grasp. She stared into the darkness, willing herself to see it. And she thought that maybe, for an instant, she caught a glimpse of it. Maybe not.

Standing at the invisible edge of her elevator roof, she looked upward for the cable of the next elevator and followed it downward with her eyes. Where it faded out of sight into darkness, her eyes followed an imaginary line down—until it was directly in front of her face. She stretched both hands in front of her and jumped off the elevator roof into the empty shaft.

Juliano and Merced stared at the radar screen.

"At first I thought it was a heavy fog bank," Merced said, "but it ain't moving."

"Oh, shit!" Juliano said, as it finally occurred to him. "Saint Martin!" He scanned the horizon with

night vision binoculars for a sign of the island. He
saw nothing.

"He must be stopping us at a harbor on the
island," Merced said tentatively.

"What's the heading?"

"Full at southeast one-six-five," Merced answered.
"You think that's a harbor?"

"No," Juliano responded. "We're heading for the
cliffs."

"The cliffs? He's gonna slam us into a wall?"

"How long before we hit?" a voice asked behind
them.

They whirled around to face Alex.

"Get back with the other passengers," Juliano
ordered. "We're moving you all to a safe deck."

"How long do we got?" Alex insisted.

Juliano drew himself up and said, "I'm the first
officer and I'm responsible for the passengers, and
you're—"

"I'm a cop and I can help," Alex said evenly. "If
you don't have control of the autopilot, there has to
be a hardwire link to Engine Control."

Juliano continued trying to stare him down,
before replying, "It's being run by remote. There's
nothing you can do—"

"We can find the transmitter," Alex interrupted.
"The stun grenades and smoke canisters were
planted in the air ducts. They were probably no
bigger than golf balls." He paused for a few seconds. "I know who it is," he continued with quiet

certainty. "His name is Geiger. Find out his cabin number. We can get this guy."

"We're not armed," Merced cautioned.

"That's where we start," Alex said briskly.


"Just pipe down, everybody!" Debbie shouted above the panicked hubbub in the corridors where they were trapped between the sealed fire doors. "Harvey was in the construction business. He'll find a way out. Just give him a chance."

Harvey looked at his wife in surprise. "Thanks a lot, Debbie," he said in an undertone.

"You can do it, sweetie!" she said to him.

Harvey ran his eyes over all the surfaces around him, feeling everybody looking at him expectantly. They were depending on him for an idea. That was fine, and he knew Debbie was proud of him being the center of attention and all that. The trouble was, he didn't have any ideas, and the more he ran his eyes over all the surfaces around him, with everybody watching, the scarcer ideas seemed to get.

As usual, Debbie read what was on his mind. "How about the ceiling, hon?" she suggested.

Harvey looked up at the fireproof insulation tiles set on metal frames. It wouldn't do any harm to take a look, he supposed. It would get him out of this tight spot anyway. "Who's lightest here?" he asked. "You can sit on my shoulders and raise some of those tiles." His look rested on Sheri.

She stepped forward to volunteer. As she passed Debbie she smirked and said, "You know, I have no underwear on."

"Then you're not sitting on Harvey's neck!" Debbie shot back. She stepped up to Harvey and made him bend double so that Sheri could stand on his back.

Sheri kicked off her shoes and was assisted onto Harvey's back.

"Damn!" Harvey moaned. "You might at least have taken your shoes off."

"I *did* take my shoes off," Sheri claimed. "Those are my knees on your back."

"They feel like wooden clogs crushing my vertebrae," Harvey complained. "You got some bony knees, lady."

"Don't worry," Sheri said in an offended voice, "this is the closest you'll ever come to them."

She got to her feet on his back and lifted aside five of the insulation tiles. All that could be seen was wiring and pipes and a solid steel ceiling above. Sheri climbed down.

"Take a look, Harvey," Debbie said, figuring that his expert eye might see something they'd missed.

"I can't straighten my back," Harvey groaned. "None of you behemoths are using me as a stepladder again."

"This is no time for playacting, Harvey," Debbie said strictly. "We need help."

"Oooooohh!" he said, his eyes closed in agony as

he forced his body into an erect position. Then he looked up at the wires in the ceiling gaps. "I was a roofer," he said, "not an electrician."

Knowing it wouldn't be long before abuse and insults started coming his way, Harvey took a walk down the corridor. He didn't know what to do about their situation. Neither did they. But they could stop picking on him. This kind of stuff had nothing to do with roofing.

Harvey stood stock-still. He looked at the air-conditioning vent a second time. There was no mistaking it. A large curl of white smoke was wafting into the corridor from it. The stuff didn't look like real smoke, more like something that came from a can, like that artificial whipped cream. But it was smoke and it was coming in. Farther down the corridor he saw more coming in another vent. Then he heard the others' voices and knew they had seen it too, from a vent nearer them. He walked back.

Debbie hurried to meet him. "Harvey, lift the carpet," she said, with a glint in her eye. "We're going to tunnel out!"

Alex, Juliano, and Merced walked quickly along a corridor and stopped outside a cabin door. Alex motioned to the two officers to stand on either side of the door while he faced it, holding the skeet-shoot gun barrel up. Alex kicked in the door in a single try.

Gun leveled, he ran inside the cabin and peered into the bathroom. Both were empty. A laptop computer was on the desk and in operation. The officers were about to follow him into the cabin when Alex put up his hand for them to stop. He listened at the door of the built-in closet. Leveling the gun on the door with one hand, he used his other hand to turn the doorknob and pull it open. A body fell out face first and crashed to the floor. The shock almost caused Alex to discharge his weapon.

With his foot, Alex turned over the body, which was bound tightly in rope. He pulled the gag from the mouth and used it to wipe blood from the face. The eyes opened.

"Why is everyone trying to kill me?" Ashton asked in an aggrieved tone.

As Alex released Ashton and helped him to his feet, Merced tried to gain access to the autopilot through the laptop. "I can't override," he said in frustration. "He changed the damn codes."

Juliano was standing in the bathroom door, looking in disgust at the leeches swimming in the bathtub. "Jesus! This guy is sick," he said.

"Exactly," a voice said loudly.

Alex whirled with the gun . . . but Geiger was not there.

The voice continued, coming from the laptop: "You think I'd be doing this if I still had my health? If I was still working for those thankless bastards?"

Alex noticed a tiny video camera plugged into

the laptop. He turned around so he wouldn't be seen by the camera and motioned silently for Juliano, Merced, and Ashton to leave the cabin. They did not need further urging.

Facing the laptop once more, Alex said, "I know who you are."

"Yeah, well, I know you, too," Geiger's voice came back. He said this as he finished dumping diamonds from lockboxes in the vault into his bag. For some moments he watched Alex on the small screen of his handheld computer. Then, with his index finger, he keyboarded in a rapid series of instructions.

When he was finished he said, "See, Alex, I designed this whole autopilot system. My company sold it to almost every shipping line in the world. But when I got sick, they just fired me."

Alex suspected something and was backing away, looking warily around him.

"I had no defense—they threw me away," Geiger continued. "So now . . . I use a more aggressive defense system."

Data rolled on Geiger's handheld computer screen and then came to a stop like the rolling elements in a slot machine. A single word was spelled across the screen: READY.

Alex could still spot nothing suspicious in the cabin, but he was as wary now as a big cat.

"Tell me, Alex," Geiger said lingeringly, savoring the moment, "do you ever have a false sense of security?"

Alex's eyes went to the laptop screen. Something was appearing there—two words: GOOD-BYE, ALEX.

He knew that somewhere a trigger was being pulled, and threw himself facedown on the floor.

The laptop exploded in a brilliant sheet of flame that spread across the cabin, even searing the corridor wall outside the cabin door.

As soon as the flame died down, Juliano, Merced, and Ashton ran through the smoke into the cabin and pulled Alex out. The flame had singed the hair on the back of his head, but otherwise Alex was all right, apart from a little deafness in both ears.

"Jesus Christ! What kind of cop are you?" Juliano shouted at him in genuine anger now that he knew Alex was unhurt. "You're gonna get the rest of us killed!"

"That's Geiger's idea, not mine," Alex said calmly. "Where's Engine Control?"

"You don't learn," Juliano said dismissively. "Let's get back to the bridge." To Ashton he said, "You, join the passengers on the upper deck."

Ashton headed off along a passageway.

"We'll stop the ship and then we'll stop Geiger," Alex told them. "I'll find Engine Control myself."

"Mr. Merced, go with him," Juliano said wearily.

"Sir, he's upset—highly irrational," Merced said nervously.

"You're an officer on this ship," Juliano reminded him. "Don't let him touch a goddamn thing."

Merced unwillingly followed the gun-toting passenger who believed he was an LAPD cop.

Annie put a blanket around the shoulders of an older woman who was among the group of badly shaken passengers she was leading to the observation deck.

Celeste caught up with her. "Annie, they won't organize a search," she said. "But I know Drew didn't get away. She's got to be here somewhere."

As Celeste spoke, Annie thought she heard the sound of muffled banging. "What's that?" she asked.

Dante pointed to a stairwell. "It's coming from down there," he said.

Annie headed for the stairwell. Achieving a sudden, miraculous recovery from his exhaustion, Dante checked his camera and followed her. At the end of the staircase they stopped and listened at a sealed fire door, but heard nothing. Then both Annie and Dante hammered on the door and waited for a reply. They heard banging on the other side!

Alex Shaw (Jason Patric) and Annie Porter
(Sandra Bullock) enjoy the start of the cruise—
before it goes out of control.

John Geiger (Willem Dafoe) reprograms the computers to set the ship on a dangerous course.

Jason Patric as Alex Shaw.

Many lives hang in the balance as lifeboats are perilously lowered from the *Seabourn Legend*.

Desperate to save the ship, Navigator Merced
(Brian McCardie), Annie, and First Officer Juliano
(Temuera Morrison) try to crack Geiger's
computer codes.

Drew (Christine Firkins) relaxes on deck while the cruise is still smooth sailing.

Dante (Royale Watkins) pulls Alex aboard after a dangerous underwater mission to stop the ship.

Geiger forces Annie down the stairs.

Alex dives out the window.

Annie is Geiger's hostage in the hair-raising final
speedboat chase scene.

"Anybody in there?" Annie shouted.

"We're trapped!" a voice yelled back, which she recognized as Frank's.

"Get us the hell out of here!" That was Sheri, of bandstand fame.

Annie was less concerned about them than about Drew. "Is there a little girl in there?" she shouted.

"No little girls here! Only big women!" A pause. "Heh-heh. Normal-sized women!" That was Harvey. "Come on, get us out of here!"

"We're trying," Annie shouted encouragingly.

She and Dante wrestled with the door, threw their shoulders against it and quickly gave it up as hopeless.

"There's smoke coming in through the vents." Liza's loud and plaintive voice came clearly through the steel door.

Annie and Dante exchanged a glance, a wordless recognition that this was where the vocally high-profile entertainment director had been confined in relative silence. Referring to the vents, Dante yelled, "Try and block them!"

Smoke was really pouring into the corridor now through several vents. Block them? Debbie started to take off her blouse.

"Deb, what do you think you're doing?" Harvey asked in an affronted tone.

"We need to block the smoke," Debbie said, explaining the obvious.

"No, wait!" Constance protested. She leaned into

the smoke issuing from the nearby air vent and deeply inhaled it.

"Constance, no!" her husband called to her.

Isabel couldn't understand it. She nudged Alejandro and said, "She's breathing smoke!"

"Hang on!" Annie's voice called confidently in. "We'll get you out!"

"How?" Dante asked her. "What do we do?"

Annie had no idea, but she was sure she would think of something. Looking around, she saw a crowbar in a shattered firebox, pulled it out and handed it to Dante. "Try this," she said.

"It's not going to work," Dante said.

"Try it," Annie insisted. "I'll find something else."

For two awful seconds Drew felt herself flying outward into dark emptiness—and then she banged straight into the heavy cable supporting the elevator next to the one she'd been in. She clutched it tightly with both hands and held it firmly between her knees. The cable was covered with heavy grease, and she felt herself begin to slip slowly downward. No matter how tightly she held on, the cable just ran through her hands and knees. She was terrified at first but then realized she could keep her descent at a very slow rate by squeezing as tightly as she could on the cable. This was exactly what she needed to do.

It seemed to take forever. Eventually she found

herself down in the sub-sub-basement somewhere, a place she'd never even thought about being on a ship. What the hell was wrong with everyone? Where were they? Well, she reasoned, this was better at least than having the elevator suddenly shoot upward beneath her and put her through the glass at the top of the shaft.

Drew landed on the elevator roof with a soft thud and opened the trapdoor. She was becoming a regular elevator engineer! She lowered herself through the opening and dropped to the floor. The elevator doors were almost closed, but she managed to squeeze herself through the crack between them.

Finally she was free!

Having danced around for a while, Drew became aware of the lack of familiarity of her surroundings. This was not like being on a ship at all. The place looked more like a factory warehouse, although she had never actually been in a factory warehouse. There were lots of crates and iron things and other things that looked like they were being stored.

Half covered with disgusting heavy grease that she would probably never get out of her pores, her beautiful red dress torn and looking like something people would wipe their hands on after fixing a car engine, Drew had to admit that she was not bored.

.     .     .

Alex and Merced sprinted down the crew stairs, moving toward the bottom of the ship. They burst through double doors that led to the Engine Control room. The place looked like the NASA space program's Mission Control at Houston, with endless control panels and digital displays. Merced took a seat in front of a computer and keyboarded stuff in.

"Which one of these runs the autopilot?" Alex asked.

"I'm not really sure," Merced answered, preoccupied with what he was doing. "Computers run everything nowadays. We don't have to operate most of it. I don't know which is which."

Alex grabbed a large wrench off a table. "What about this one?" he asked, smashing a control panel with a blow from the wrench.

Merced clicked on his radio and spoke urgently into it: "Sir, this is Merced in Engine Control—he's beating up on the equipment!"

Alex smashed a computer screen and a digital display.

Merced, staring at the busted electronics, continued speaking into his radio in a low, urgent voice: "Come in, Juliano! Does anyone read me?"

"There must be something that's not hooked up to the computers," Alex suggested, swinging the wrench idly. He was wearing the skeet gun by its strap on his back.

"There's plenty," Mercedes answered, "but nothing that can help us."

"What are these switches?" Alex asked, pointing. He looked at a label and read, "Open ballast release—"

"Don't touch that!" Merced practically squealed. "You want to flood the bottom of the ship? Those open the ballast doors. They can't help us." Merced motioned to a video monitor that showed a closed door. "There's nothing we can do," he said. "Geiger locked us out. We can't stop or steer the ship."

"Then we'll have to slow it down," Alex suggested.

"Slow it down?" Merced looked at him like he was demented. "What are you gonna do, let the air out of her tires?"

"No," Alex said sweetly. "We're gonna open the ballast doors . . . just like you said."

Alex moved toward the switches. Merced jumped in front of him, blocking his way. "What are you talking about?" he asked, trying to delay this disturbed person.

"You said if we open the doors, we flood the bottom of the ship," Alex explained patiently. "That should slow us down."

"I never said that!" Merced declared, the pitch of his voice rising. "If she takes on too much water, we all go down."

Alex only smiled at him.

Merced clicked on his radio and spoke urgently once more into it: "This is Merced to Bridge. Does—"

Alex snapped the radio from Merced's hand. He nodded toward the switches. "Flood it," he ordered.

. . .

By now all the women had donated their blouses, and all the men their shirts, to blocking the air vents. The clothes helped prevent smoke from leaking into the corridor in which they were trapped. But they had not used enough clothes to block all the smoke.

Debbie looked at her husband. "Harvey," she said, "give me your pants."

"My pants?" he pleaded. "Nobody else has taken off their pants."

"I took off my pants," Alejandro said, displaying an athletic build in jockey shorts. Most of the others had looked a lot better with their clothes on.

"Look, my father was a Methodist deacon," Harvey explained. "I just can't take off my pants."

Meanwhile Constance drifted over to the nearest vent issuing smoke and inhaled a lungful.

"Would you mind blowing that in another direction," Liza said sharply as Constance exhaled. "People are trying to breathe here."

Frank, Constance's husband, stuffed his shirt in the vent. "It's still coming through," he observed.

"Your pants, Harvey!" Debbie demanded. "Give me your goddamn pants!"

Harvey pointed at Sheri Silver and said, "I want to know why she hasn't taken off a thing."

"Because I'm not wearing any underwear," Sheri told him.

Harvey gave in and pulled off his pants.

• • •

Merced's hand shook as he hit the series of switches marked CARGO OPEN.

"Can you do this any faster?" Alex urged.

"I've never let a million gallons of water into a ship before," Merced protested. "Give me a second."

Merced opened cargo doors 1 and 2, and two of the screens on the series of monitors showed these doors begin to open and seawater flooding in.

"Okay, it's coming in," Merced said. "We should get out of here."

Alex took one last look at the series of monitors to make sure the water was coming in. As he watched, Drew entered one screen, walked out of it and was picked up on another. He realized that she could not hear the sound of inrushing water. By the time she saw the water, it might be too late for her to save herself.

"Close it!" Alex yelled. "Close it!"

"What?" Merced asked. He still hadn't seen Drew on the screens. "You just told me to open them." Then he saw her and rushed to the switches to undo what he'd done. Slowly, the doors began to close against the pressure of incoming seawater.

Still wearing his tuxedo, and with the skeet gun still strapped to his back, Alex rushed down the stairs that he guessed led to the cargo hold. He guessed right and soon found himself rushing around among stacks of cargo. He could hear the gurgle of water echoing from somewhere in the vast cargo hold. Drew needed to see him, or he had to see her, before it was too late.

He turned a corner and saw her not far away. She was standing frozen as a huge surge of water rolled toward her. He lunged forward and grabbed her under one arm. Then he tried to outrun the water surge. The water broke over them just before he reached a stairwell, but Alex managed to get a grip on a handrail and hung on. Once the first powerful wave of water had hit them and passed, he headed up the stairs, setting down Drew on her feet in front of him. The water level was rising fast. He did not have to tell her to move up the steps as fast as she could.

Geiger's handheld computer started to beep. He glanced at the screen and saw a graphic of the ship with a red line indicating an area in the bottom. Words flashed on and off: FLOODING IN SECTION 7C. PROGRAM CHANGED.

Geiger put down his sack of diamonds and keyboarded in some data. The screen prompted: INSTALL MODIFIED PROGRAM? He keyboarded some more.

Smoke still poured in through the air vents, though they were stuffed with clothes. It was becoming increasingly difficult for the trapped passengers to breathe in the corridor sealed off by unopenable fire doors. The half-dressed passengers used the spaces between the smoke and the walls in order to breathe.

"I've had enough," Constance said after a coughing fit. "I'll give it up. I swear I'll give it up."

"I can't breathe," Liza announced loudly.

"Hurry up!" Harvey shouted at Dante through the fire door. "I don't want to die without my pants on!"

Frank lost his patience. "For God's sake, just give this guy back his pants!"

On the other side of the big steel door, Dante wasn't making much progress with the crowbar. He didn't know whether to be hopeful or dismayed when he saw Annie coming back with a chain saw. She seemed pleased with herself.

"Maybe this will do it," she said brightly. She hit the starter and the chain saw roared to life. She held the saw out in front of her and approached the wall beside the door. As Annie cut into the wall with the saw, Dante stepped back and took photos. She cut a square about a foot across out of the wall. Smoke poured out.

"What the hell am I doing?" Annie wondered.

"Don't stop!" Dante shouted enthusiastically, happier to be working a camera than a crowbar. "Just keep hacking!"

Annie cut another adjoining section out of the

wall, so that by now there was a good-sized hole. "Can you get out?" she yelled into the hole.

Frank stuck his head out of the hole. He stared at Annie standing in front of him with the buzzing chain saw. "We'll give it a shot if you move away with that saw," he offered.

By the time Drew and Alex reached the top of the stairs, the water had risen halfway up their bodies. The level beneath was now completely filled with water. They had made it out with only seconds to spare. But they hadn't reached safety. The water continued to rise fast on the upper level where they now stood. Alex heard the sound of another rushing surge of water—there must have been a cargo door on this level too.

He grabbed Drew's hand and together they ran down a hall toward a set of double doors. But this time the water caught them long before they got near where they wanted to go. Alex held onto her hand as the onrushing cascade of water swept them with it toward the doors. The initial wave of water opened the doors and they passed through, struggling to remain upright in the flooding stream.

Looking around him, Alex saw that they were in the ship's laundry, with its oversized washing machines and dryers. He needed to find something to hang on to before they were swept against something hard, knocked senseless and drowned.

Overhead were laundry bags hanging from a kind of conveyor line. He got a grip on one bag as they were being swept by underneath. With Drew holding her arms around his neck, he slowly climbed, hand over hand, up the laundry bag to the conveyor line. Their weight was pulling the laundry bag open and a mess of socks and underwear spilled out of its unraveling top. If the bag opened fully, it might slip off the hook and they would be swept forward again. The water level continued to rise.

Getting a grip on the conveyor line, Alex unhooked the laundry bag, and in its place hooked Drew by her red dress. Then he traveled hand over hand along the line to a wall where he saw a switch just above water level. Hanging from the line by his hands, he tipped the switch down with one foot. The conveyor line began to move slowly, bearing Drew along like a prize ham.

Going back along the line, hand over hand, Alex headed toward Drew. But long before he could reach her, the conveyor line, moving across the ceiling, brought her to an opening in which hung long, flat, rubber strips. Drew screamed as the rubber strips crawled across her body. Not long after, Alex also passed through the rubber strips. They now found themselves in a large room with a dry floor. But they had a problem.

The conveyor line hooks were automatically unhooking the laundry bags ahead of them and dropping them into a huge bin filled with towels. Alex could have just let go of the conveyor line and dropped down to the floor, but Drew was firmly hooked by the dress and could not free herself in time to avoid the fate of the laundry bags. Her hook opened, and she fell with a scream, which was then muffled by the heaps of towels she landed on.

Alex struggled to hold onto the line, but his grip failed when he was over the bin, and he followed Drew onto the bed of soft terrycloth.

Annie and Dante led the shocked and exhausted smoke victims into the atrium. They had not been able to retrieve their clothes from the air vents, and now they all looked like they'd been marooned for a week on a desert isle.

"What's going on?" Sheri asked, looking around her. "Why has the evacuation stopped?"

"Stopped?" Frank said. "We don't even know why it started!"

"Are we sinking?" Debbie wanted to know.

"We got flotation cushions, don't we?" Harvey contributed. "If we can't take a lifeboat, we can still jump off the back of the ship."

"At twenty knots, that water is like concrete,"

Dante told him. "And if the impact didn't totally kill you, getting sucked into the propellers would certainly finish the job."

That shut Harvey up.

"So we're just going to die here," Sheri summed up.

"Nobody is going to die," Dante said, trying not to lose his patience. "Just calm down!"

Suddenly, Celeste's face lit up with emotion. "Drew! Drew!" she cried.

Drew, in her torn and oily red dress, and Alex, in his rumpled-beyond-repair tuxedo, skeet gun on his back, had appeared in the atrium. Both were covered with white terrycloth lint. Celeste and Rupert ran forward to meet Drew, who threw herself into her mother's arms. They hugged each other tightly.

On catching sight of the pair, Annie had stood stock-still, only able to say, "Alex!" Then she recovered and strode forward to meet him. They embraced. "What happened?" she asked. "Are you guys okay?"

"We're fine . . . I think," Alex said, caressing her. Then he stepped away and said in a serious tone, "It's Geiger. He designed the autopilot and now he's taken over."

"Why?" she asked.

"'Cause he's sick." Alex looked more closely at the people around them. "Why's everyone half naked?" he asked.

"Because we're having so much fun," Annie said in a good imitation of Liza, the entertainment director.

"Let's move everyone up on deck," Alex suggested.

"But everyone else is in the top lounge," Annie informed him. "We're supposed to keep together."

Alex nodded and they started to gently round up everyone. As they moved people across the atrium, they walked by a passageway at the end of which the vault door was visible. The big steel door was open. With some rapid cop reasoning, Alex figured that either some of the diamond merchants had rescued their merchandise before taking to the lifeboats, or someone had gained access to the vault and stolen their rocks. Either way, he thought, it was none of his business. Protecting the lives of the people still on board—that he saw as his duty, even if the ship's officers didn't see a role in this for him. Diamonds were never a cop's best friend.

Alex would have passed by the open vault without bothering, if a whole new series of alarms hadn't attracted his attention. That, and the light above the vault door was flashing. Something in the vault was tripping these signals.

Alex knew who it was. "That's him," he said. "Get everyone to the top of the ship, now!"

"Alex," Annie said, "you know for once you don't have to be Superman."

"I'll be right back," he promised. "Okay?"

Annie reluctantly nodded, and he ran off. She turned to the passengers nearby and called out, "Okay, we're heading to the top lounge. Everyone move!"

Heading down the passageway toward the vault, Alex lifted the skeet gun off his back and pumped a cartridge into the chamber. When he turned the corner at the vault door, the corridor was empty. A door to a stairwell was slowly swinging closed. Alex made for it and charged down the stairs, at the foot of which corridors ran left and right, both empty and layered with smoke. Alex went on gut instinct—he picked the left one and continued running hard.

The corridor led into a game room, and Alex had to dodge in and out to cross the room. As he ran, his hip caught the corner of a pinball machine, which tipped over and crashed on the floor, its electronic bells and whistles sounding loudly, its red lights flashing, a high score running on its spinning counters.

Geiger heard the pinball machine meet its end not far behind him. He looked back fearfully over his shoulder to see if Alex was gaining on him, but swirling smoke blocked his view. He knew that if he couldn't see Alex, then his pursuer couldn't see him. All he had to do was keep going, until the stupid cop made a wrong turn. Then, in a ship this size, he would have lost him for good.

Running into a large space, Geiger was momentarily confused about his whereabouts because the smoke was so thick. There were so many passenger lounges all over the place, it was easy to mix up one with another. A layer of smoke a couple of feet above the carpet concealed a glass-topped coffee table. Geiger yelped as he struck it with his shins. He brought his foot down savagely on the tabletop and shattered the glass. He was no sailor—he forgot about moving vessels locating one another in thick fog by making noise.

Alex stepped out of the thick smoke on the other side of the lounge, his skeet gun leveled.

"Drop the gun," he said to Geiger.

Geiger froze in place, staring at the gun barrel like a mesmerized rabbit. He was about forty feet away.

Alex couldn't see him clearly through the smoke. "Put your hands in the air and get on your knees," he called in his SWAT voice. "Drop the weapon!"

Geiger was backing away through an open fire door into a corridor beyond. Alex advanced fast, combat style, through the easy chairs and tables, then leveled the gun on his quarry.

Geiger froze. "Don't shoot!" he shouted. He raised his handheld computer. "It's not a gun, it's just a computer."

Alex moved closer, having difficulty seeing through the smoke. He didn't see Geiger's fingers still moving on the computer keyboard. "Drop it now, asshole!" Alex commanded.

"Where's your girlfriend, Annie?" Geiger taunted him. "Sure hope she's not still on board."

Alex sqeezed his trigger finger. The muzzle of the skeet gun spat flame, and a cone of fine skeet shot peppered the ceiling above Geiger's head. The gun blast in this enclosed space almost deafened both men. Crumbled plaster and flakes of paint rained down on Geiger's head and shoulders. From his look of terror, Alex guessed that some stray shot had punctured his skin.

Geiger now heard the unmistakably sinister scrape of metal on metal as Alex racked another cartridge into the firing chamber.

Leveling the smoking barrel at Geiger's chest, Alex said calmly and quietly, "Now, asshole!"

"Just trying to make conversation," Geiger said effusively. He held out the computer in front of him and stooped toward the floor, saying, "I'm putting this down, real slow. . . ."

As he placed the electronic device on the carpet, Geiger's forefinger pressed the ENTER key. Alex didn't even notice. In an instant the fire door swung to a three-quarters closed position between them, blocking their view of one another. The door continued closing the last few inches more slowly. Alex rushed in and wedged his shoulder in the space between the door and door frame. Then, as in an arm-wrestling contest, he met force with force and gradually pushed the door back into a half-open position.

He didn't even have to look—he knew Geiger would be gone. Alex took off after him.

• • •

As Alex ran in pursuit down the long corridor, he noticed the smoke getting thicker. That maniac Geiger had planted time-release smoke bombs all over the ship, and where he hadn't planted any, the ship's air-circulation system was doing the work for him. Geiger had claimed to know his job. From what Alex had seen so far, he'd been telling the truth. From his experience in the LAPD, Alex knew the damage smart guys caused when they went bad. A dumb guy did mostly dumb crime. An ultrasmart guy was capable of anything.

Alex knew where he was now—the ballroom. This was where Annie and he had been when the trouble first started, when the ship started shaking and shuddering, when passengers first started panicking. . . . It seemed like so long ago now, and yet he was still wearing his tuxedo, or what remained of it. Poor Annie, she'd been so looking forward to a peaceful cruise on which they could just be a normal couple together, whatever she meant by that. And, of course, she would hold him responsible, in some mysterious way, for everything that had happened—and was still happening!—on this cruise to hell. . . .

Moving through rows of tables, skeet gun at the ready, Alex peered through the thick, white smoke for any sign of movement. At one place in the smoke he saw something blurry—it looked like

Geiger's face! He aimed and fired. The image was shattered in a million pieces—he'd hit a video screen suspended from the ceiling above the dance floor! As he pumped another shell into the chamber, he saw images of Geiger's face emerge from the smoke all around him, like some horror movie version of a bad dream. Then he listened. It was getting worse. Geiger was talking to him!

"Computers made me what I am, Alex," the Geiger voices from all the ceiling video screens around him were saying. "Day and night I spent hard at work—so dedicated!—unaware of what it was doing to me."

Alex made a slow 360-degree turn, looking for a sign of the flesh-and-blood Geiger. There was nothing, except all these identical video faces and voices, floating out of the smoke at him.

"All electronics emit small electric fields," Geiger's voices were telling him in a melancholy monotone. "Over time, even the best doctors in the world don't know what they do to you. . . ."


Annie rushed onto the bridge. "Geiger robbed the vault," she said to Juliano. "Alex is trying to stop him."

Juliano put a finger to his lips for her to be quiet and pointed to the bridge address system speaker.

"The irony of my situation, Alex," Geiger said, his voice coming over the speaker, "is that dedication to job and devotion to company was repaid with a terminal illness and a pink slip. See, computers generate electromagnetic fields which over time can cause severe copper poisoning. I'm a smart guy and even I didn't know that." It was clear that Geiger was striving to rationalize the things he intended doing. He went on, "I would've really appreciated a little understanding from upper management, you know what I mean, Alex? But now I've just got to do whatever I can. Unfortunately, at any cost."

Annie ran for the door. From the way Geiger was talking, it sounded like he had the upper hand and Alex was in trouble. She had no idea of where to find Alex, but she knew he wasn't on the bridge. She'd keep going until she found him.

"Wait!" Juliano shouted, and followed her.

The smoke in the ballroom was so dense, Alex had trouble breathing. He poured a pitcher of water over a small tablecloth and held that over his nose and mouth. It helped filter out some of the smoke, which was already making his throat feel raw. He had to get out of here. Next to the bandstand he saw an exit sign. A fire door started to close in front of him, but he was too quick for it and passed through, allowing it to shut behind him. He interpreted that as a sign that Geiger did not want him to come this way.

Alex found himself in the shopping arcade,

which had already closed for the night when the troubles began. It was essentially a large space lined with stores, now locked with security gates. The smoke was much thinner here, and Alex lifted the wet tablecloth from his face and gratefully inhaled deep drafts of air.

He was still getting his bearings when he heard something to one side of him. It was a fire door swinging open automatically. Was Geiger issuing an invitation to him? Well, Alex thought, he would gratefully accept.

Skeet gun ready, he eased into the open door. It led to a storeroom lined with shelves of liquor bottles. No one was inside. At the far end was a security door with a circular glass porthole in its upper half. Alex could see that the door was open a few inches, and he made for it. As soon as he did, the steel fire door closed behind him. Then, before he could reach it, the security door was slammed shut in front of him. He was trapped. Something from outer space peered through the glass porthole at him. Then this creature peeled the gas mask off its face. It was Geiger.

"How are you gonna stop me now, my friend?" Geiger shouted through the door.

Alex answered in the simplest and most direct way he could think of. He took quick aim at the face in the glass porthole and squeezed off a shot. The glass was bulletproof. The light shot used for skeet shooting not only didn't crack the glass, it didn't even scratch it. Alex pumped the gun for another try. It was empty. He cast it aside.

But he'd frightened the shit out of Geiger. When Geiger next peered through the porthole, he couldn't conceal his fear and shock; it showed in his face. Alex laughed at him. Geiger saw himself being mocked, and in an instant his face was transformed into a mask of hate. Wielding his handheld computer like a pistol, Geiger aimed it through the glass in Alex's direction and pressed a key.

A stun grenade exploded on a shelf behind Alex. He threw himself to the floor, and was unhurt. The grenade broke a number of liquor bottles and ignited an alcohol fire too large for Alex to attempt to put out. He needed to get out of here, but there was nothing in the storeroom to break the security-door glass.

He looked back at the door. Geiger was smiling in at him. He held up a grenade for Alex to see and then wedged it somewhere at the bottom of the door. He wanted Alex to know that even if he did somehow get the door open, he would have to meet the force of this grenade. At the other end, the steel fire door was sealed tight. And the flames among the liquor bottles were getting higher.

As he waved good-bye to Alex through the glass, Geiger had a look of mock sympathy that made Alex grind his teeth.

●    ●    ●

Annie stopped, hearing the explosion of the stun grenade on the shelf of liquor bottles, but not knowing what it was or where the sound came from.

"Did you hear that?" she asked Juliano.

"This way," he said.

While they were heading in the direction Juliano thought the sound had come from, Alex edged past the flames back into the storeroom in search of something that would help him in his predicament. The flames were way out of control. He had to open one of those doors. He saw a row of switches on the wall and rapidly pressed them all down. The only result was that the awful mall music started to play. He didn't have time to shut the damn stuff off, because he had to get back to the security door before the rising flames cut off the way. The heat was searing as he ran past the flames. At the security door, he suddenly felt dizzy and weak. He tried to lean on the door for support but slipped down on his knees and then lay on the floor.

Annie and Juliano were in the atrium, looking around in the thick smoke.

"Wait," Annie said. "I've heard that music before."

Juliano shrugged. It sounded to him like the calypso music he heard every day. "It's the music they pipe in all over the ship," he said. "It could be anywhere."

"No," Annie said firmly. "I *know* that music." She

listened some more, and then it came to her. She said, "It's shopping music. He's in the mall!"

"This way," Juliano said.

As they rushed toward the mall area, Geiger heard their approaching voices and footsteps. He slipped into a cabin and waited for them to run by. While he waited, he checked the screen of his handheld computer. A graphic showed the state of flooding in the cargo holds of the ship. A message ran: FLOODING WILL CANCEL PROGRAM, CAPTAIN. REPROGRAM OR CANCEL?

Geiger thought for a moment and then keyboarded the following onto the screen: REPROGRAM FOR WEIGHT AND BALLAST CHANGES. He pressed the ENTER key. The words on the screen were replaced by a digital clock that began counting down from 39:13 . . . 39:12 . . .

Annie and Juliano spent a little time looking around the mall and had wandered out again when Annie's eye caught the flickering light in the glass porthole of the security door. She looked through it and saw the roaring fire. Had she not glanced down, she might have missed seeing Alex's body prone on the floor just inside the door.

"Alex!" she shouted, hammering on the glass.

He looked up at her but seemed too weak or overcome to get to his feet.

"Shit!" Annie said in frustration. "I need my saw!"

"It's okay," Juliano said. "I have a key." He went to turn it in the lock, but stopped when he looked in and saw Alex, now on his knees, feverishly gesturing him away.

"Don't touch it!" Alex yelled with all his remaining strength. He pointed toward the bottom of the door at one side.

At first they thought he meant something on his side of the door.

"Oh, God!" Annie said when she saw the grenade only inches away from her, wedged so that the door opening would knock it loose on the floor. She looked in the porthole again and saw that Alex had sunk back to the floor. His eyes were closed. She could see that the flames were growing higher among the bottles. She rapped hard with her knuckles on the glass and called, "Alex! Wake up! Tell me what to do!"

He opened his eyes and looked up at her. She had to put her ear to the glass to hear what he said.

"What does it say on the front?" he asked.

She knew he had to be talking about the grenade, as if she could tell the front from the back of a thing like that. She looked at it. "L-1696," she read.

"Is the pin out?" he asked.

"I don't know." She turned to Juliano. "Is the pin out?"

"I think so," he said.

"You're going to have to tie the spoon to the grenade," Alex told them.

Annie looked at the grenade and wondered what he was talking about. "Spoon?" she asked. "What spoon?"

"Tie it with a shoelace," Alex said.

Annie looked at her shoes. "My shoes don't have laces," she said. She pointed to Juliano's. "Give me your shoes!" she demanded.

Glancing in at the flames through the porthole, Juliano hurriedly pulled off one shoe and ripped the lace out of it. He handed it to Annie.

"Okay, I've got a lace," she reported to Alex. "I see something that looks like a little spoon—"

"Tie it across the top," Alex instructed.

Annie's hands were shaking as she gingerly wrapped the shoelace around the grenade. "Okay, I'm putting the lace around this thing," she reported. She tied it from bottom to top, pulled the lace tight and put a neat bow on the top. "Okay. I tied it," she said. "Now what?"

Alex opened his eyes, fighting to stay conscious now. With a weaker voice he called, "Slowly pull it out . . ."

Annie put her hand on the grenade and pulled it out slowly from where it was wedged. As she nervously held it in her hand to one side of the door, a wall of liquor bottles exploded behind Alex. The blast rolled over him and knocked the security door off its hinges. Annie was lifted up by the blast and thrown several feet. She screamed as she landed flat on her back. But like a fallen outfielder holding on to the baseball after a dramatic catch, she didn't let the grenade drop to the floor.

"Where is it?" she asked.

"It's in your hand," Juliano said.

Annie looked and saw that he was right. "Would you mind taking it from me?" she asked.

Juliano very carefully took the grenade from her hand and delicately placed it on the floor.

"Thanks," Annie said.

Annie and Juliano had to help Alex to his feet and lead him, coughing, choking, and trying to catch his breath, out into the fresh sea air. He collapsed against the deck rail and breathed the cool night air in and out, getting oxygen back into his bloodstream. Some more hair on the back of his head had been singed, and his tuxedo was hardly recognizable as such anymore—but otherwise he wasn't too badly off, considering what he'd been through.

Annie found a wooden upright chair and said, "Sit right here. Don't get up. Don't move."

Alex reluctantly sat, saying, "I'm okay."

"Stop saying that. You're not okay," Annie responded. "Are you okay?"

The sun was beginning to peep over the horizon to the east, a pink glow marking the line between sky and sea. Weatherwise, it looked like the start of another perfect Caribbean day. The dawn looked so tranquil and pretty, it would have been easy for Annie and Alex to forget all the mishaps they had experienced, if it weren't for the undeniable fact that the ship was moving at full speed toward some unknown destination under the control of a loony killer who was still at liberty somewhere on board. Even the most rosy-fingered dawn couldn't make them forget something like that.

Alex tried to focus his eyes on something that he thought he could see ahead of the ship in the spreading light. It was definitely land, a Caribbean island. Annie and Juliano followed his line of sight and saw it too. All three were staring at it when they felt the ship make a sudden alteration.

Juliano had to steady himself. "Did you feel that?" he asked. "He's adjusting the course."

"Around the island?" Annie asked hopefully.

"More like right into it," Juliano said dolefully.

"Alex, get up," Annie said. "We have to stop the ship."


In the bar, the warmest and most comfortable place on the observation deck, Celeste and Rupert huddled on a banquette with their teenage daughter. Drew looked depressed and beyond tired. All three were clad in the rags of their former clothes.

Liza was standing near one of the big observation windows. "I've never been so scared," she was saying in her loud voice. "I really felt like death in that place. You know what I'm saying?"

"I'm not listening to you," Sheri said shortly.

"I don't understand you," Liza said. "You're in the entertainment business. Show biz! Yet all you do is sit around and worry about your agent and bookings."

"If you *had* an agent or bookings, you'd worry too," Sheri said acidly. "You're just a kindergarten teacher gone wrong."

"How could you say such a thing to me?"

"Easy!" Sheri said.

"If you were any good as a musician, you'd be in Las Vegas or New York, not on a cruise ship," Liza retorted.

"I expect you're right," Sheri said wearily.

This was not the reply Liza had been expecting. Now she felt guilty for having said something horrid to a fellow worker. "I'm sorry!" she exclaimed. "I shouldn't have said that. I don't know what came over me!"

"Liza, please leave me alone."

"We might die here," Liza said in a sudden change of tone. "I'm scared."

"Liza, I want to die alone."

Debbie was nearby with her husband, in his underpants, and with Ashton, looking out the big window at the sunrise on the sea. "Harvey, look, an island!" Debbie said. "We're going to be saved."

Harvey squinted out over the bright water. "You have an eagle eye, babe," he said. "That's land, no doubt about it. Next we'll be seeing palm trees and coconuts on the beach. We could be castaways on this island for many years."

"I hope it has a casino," Debbie said.

"We could be self-sufficient," Harvey went on. "Elect a leader among ourselves, live on fruit and nuts—"

"Shut up, Harvey," Debbie said. "You'd have to make us all palm-thatch roofs and dig wells. Your back would give out."

Harvey shook his head. "I'd have a new lease on life."

"Anyway, I see buildings on this island," Debbie said, relieved to find that it was not some kind of deserted coral atoll.

Harvey walked to the window and examined the island. "Is that a harbor?" he asked Ashton.

"Thank God," Ashton said, nodding. He had been silently praying. His prayers were being answered. "We're heading into port . . . we'll be fine. I'll go see how long before we can get off this ship."

Annie and Alex were on the bridge with Juliano and Merced. All the animosity was gone between the ship's officers and Alex. They were glad of his presence now. The sun was coming up over the island of St. Martin. Annie watched the land through binoculars. Alex stared at the screen of the main computer, while Juliano and Merced fiddled with the steering program.

"It doesn't make sense," Juliano said. "If Geiger's setting a direct course, then why flood the bottom of the ship?"

"He didn't flood it," Alex said.

Juliano turned to Alex. "What?"

Merced nervously stepped away from Juliano, who looked at him and asked, "You opened the cargo doors?"

Merced swallowed. "Let me say, sir, that—"

"You want to kill us all?" Juliano asked incredulously.

"Forget the cargo doors. They're closed," Alex put in. "How long before we hit this island?"

As Juliano and Merced did some rapid calculations, Annie scanned with the binoculars. Suddenly, something big and out of focus in the foreground interrupted her view of the island. She focused on this object and could hardly believe her eyes—it was a massive supertanker anchored off the island and directly in the *Seabourn Legend*'s present path.

"Guys, we're not gonna hit that island," Annie announced.

They all turned to look. Juliano studied the radar screen and then took the binoculars from Annie. After looking through them, he said, "That's an oil tanker, and he's taking us right into it—"

"Just like he planned," Alex put in.

Juliano estimated they were about fifteen miles from where the tanker was anchored. He said the vessel was a thousand feet long, weighed over 300,000 tons, and was loaded with oil. It would dwarf the largest cruise ship in the world. On the side of the tanker, as seen through binoculars, were huge letters: STENA CONVOY.

They felt a slight shift as the ship changed course.

"He's turning us," Merced said, checking the compass. "Two degrees starboard."

Both he and Juliano became increasingly agitated as they moved between the radar screen and various navigational computers.

"She's sixteen miles out," Merced estimated. "We're doing twenty-six knots."

This meant little to Annie, but she was picking up on their apprehension. "They'll see us, right?" she asked. "They'll get their ship out of the way?"

"She's anchored," Juliano answered in a hangdog way, "which means that even when they do see us, it's going to take at least thirty minutes for them to move that thing."

Alex asked, "Can we turn the ship with the bow thrusters?"

"There's no way to get there," Juliano said. "You two flooded it!"

Merced was back at the compass. "He's moving us another quarter," he announced.

"That's why he hasn't jumped ship yet," Alex said. "He's lining us up."

"The flooding must have screwed up his program," Merced said in agreement. Getting in a dig at Juliano, he added, "Just like we thought it would."

Annie was tired of all this talk. "There must be something we can do," she suggested.

"There is," Alex replied. "We have to stop the propeller."

"The blades on that thing are ten feet across," Juliano told him. "They'll kill you."

Merced put in, "Sir, you could wedge something into the drive shaft—" He stopped when he got the evil eye from his senior officer. "Not that I'm suggesting this," he added lamely.

"Let's go," Alex said.

Juliano said to Merced, "You stay on the bridge." Then he followed close behind Alex and Annie in her tattered evening gown. This time he intended to be around to nip any wild schemes in the bud.


On the bridge of the anchored supertanker, two officers played Trivial Pursuit. One asked, "What part did actor Gary Burghoff play on *M\*A\*S\*H*?"

The other officer was not concentrating on the game. He became distracted by something on the radar screen. Getting to his feet, he walked over to it. There was a dot on the screen—a moving dot. It was approaching their position.

After Drew's experience, and on his own as a cop, Alex knew better then to chance an elevator, although it was a long way down from the ship's bridge to its lower depths. It was also not easy to find one's way, except that it was always downward.

Juliano gave him directions. "Down the next stairwell. Straight to the bowels of the ship."

"Bowels?" Annie said. "That doesn't sound good."

"How much time do we have?" Alex asked.

Checking his watch, Juliano said, "Just hurry."

Geiger, with his black bag tied to his waist, headed for the marina at the back of the ship. He glanced down at the screen of his handheld computer: 26:04.

On the sky deck, the passengers had noticed the supertanker in the distance, anchored off the island, and gathered at a window to view it. Dante used a telescopic lens to take souvenir photos of the scene.

Ruby asked, "You think that ship is going to rescue us?"

"What else could it be?" Harvey answered.

Back on the bridge, Merced was sending out an SOS on the radio. "Mayday! Mayday! This is the *Seabourn Legend*. Bearing seventeen degrees southeast. Steering and engine controls nonfunctional, I repeat, nonfunctional."

Ashton came on the bridge while he was sending this message. He was first alarmed by the message—and then even more alarmed when he saw Merced put down the transmitter in disgust. It was clear that the radio was also nonfunctional.

"Where are we going?" Ashton asked.

Merced ignored him, looking out the window at the supertanker and again picking up the radio transmitter. "Come in *Stena Convoy*," he said. "This is the *Seabourn Legend*. Come in, *Stena Convoy*."

As Ashton looked through the window and saw the anchored tanker, closer now than a few minutes ago, the situation began to dawn on him. "You're kidding," he said, hoping someone might be. When the stark truth sank home, he said, "I should've been a flight attendant."


Annie, Alex, and Juliano were in the loading dock on the starboard side of the ship. Juliano opened a huge sliding door in the ship's side, only about ten feet above the waterline, and they looked out at the ocean speeding by. Toward the back of the ship, the water raged and churned.

The loading dock was filled with all kinds of heavy and light equipment. Alex selected a flexible steel mooring cable and a scuba outfit. Annie helped him into the wetsuit and flippers, and held the oxygen tank for him to place on his back.

While Juliano paid out a length of mooring cable from a power winch, Annie helped Alex attach a much lighter safety cable to his waist. The safety cable was controlled by its own light winch. They stood at the open loading dock door, looking down at the seawater sweeping beneath them.

"Alex, maybe this isn't such a hot idea," Annie said, overcome by fears for her loved one. "Maybe we should just leave the propeller alone."

"We have to stop the ship," Alex said, logically enough.

"Not too much slack on the safety line," Juliano cautioned Annie. "We don't want to cut him in half."

This didn't make Annie feel any better. She looked at the safety cable doubtfully and asked, "You sure this will hold?"

"We use those lines all over the ship," Juliano assured her.

"He's not going all over the ship," she pointed out. "He's going under the ship."

"Annie, it's okay," Alex said. "It'll hold." He took her in his arms and kissed her. Pulling away, he quickly put his mask on.

Annie hitched up her evening gown and grabbed the safety line.

Lifting his mask, Alex said, "Remember 4296–589J."

"What are you talking about?" Annie asked.

He said, "My badge number is 4296–589J." Their eyes met, and he gave her a quick smile before pulling on the mask once more, checking his oxygen supply and diving backward into the water.

Annie watched nervously as the safety line ran off the winch spool.

"Annie, he's close enough," Juliano said. "Stop him now."

She pushed the stop button on the winch.

Alex plunged into the swirling, bubbling, powerful currents that pulled him this way and that beneath the huge underside of the ship. He tried to use his flippers to kick clear of the ship, so as not to be injured or pressed up against it and immobilized by the pressure of moving water. That was easier said than done. He took several hard knocks against the ship's bottom before he learned how he had to stay in constant motion, kicking strongly, to keep himself clear.

Most of all, he found it hard to see, with all the turbulence and bubbles in the water. And when the water set him spinning on his safety line, like a fishing lure, he soon lost his sense of up and down—

only to be forcibly reminded when he hit the underside. That was up!

He tried to hold on to the mooring cable but lost hold of it as he was being knocked about, then found it, only to lose it again. He could tell this wasn't going to work. It was way beyond what he'd expected. He was like a bean in a food processor. Maybe that was why Juliano hadn't argued against him doing this, expecting this would finally quiet him down, or maybe finish him off. This thought was enough to get Alex going again. He would show the ship's senior officer. The guy made his living on board this ship, Alex thought, but so far as he was concerned, the dude still had things to learn from the LAPD. And he was the one who would teach him.

He kicked with his flippers and peered through the bubble-laden pale green water for the trailing mooring cable. The bubbles often pressed against the outside of his glass visor like flattened, shape-less amoebas before slithering away. Then he saw the long, black, snaking form of the cable in the sunlit water. It had moved out about fifteen or twenty feet from the ship, where the water was at its most turbulent. The woven steel cable was being flicked back and forth, as if it were light as a cob-web. Any of those flicks would have taken a gob of flesh off his bones, along with a patch of wetsuit.

There was nothing he could do but wait for the intertwining currents to bring the cable in closer to the ship's underside, where the flow of water was smoother and the cable stopped behaving like a steel-thonged bullwhip. He caught hold of it once more. It felt like a writhing muscular snake in his hands, curling, vibrating, wriggling. He held on.

Once he was in control of the mooring cable, he tried to move farther back along the ship's underside, pulling it with him, but his own safety line would not permit this. Alex cursed, then grinned, guessing that Annie was controlling his leash and that he was not going to get any more. Instead, he pulled hard on the mooring line, and after a few seconds felt it being released. Juliano was probably paying it out from the power winch as he pulled. Alex looked behind him and saw that the loose end of the mooring cable was staying close to the underside. He guessed that he himself was about a hundred feet in front of the propeller. The cable stretched about twenty feet behind him. Therefore, eighty pulls or so should bring the end of the mooring cable into contact with the propeller. Alex was not quite sure what would happen then, but he had high hopes.

He yanked on the cable, keeping count as he did so. When he figured that the cable end must be very close to the whirling blades of the propeller, he tried to keep the cable at arm's length from his body. He pulled on the cable now as hard as he could, then suddenly felt tremors run through the woven cable as it became entangled in the screw blades. Getting his hands off it quickly, he kicked away on his safety line as the revolving propeller started to pull cable off the winch at high speed.

On the loading dock, Annie and Juliano watched the mooring cable fly off the winch and speed across the floor, raising sparks as it scraped on steel. The cable disappeared through the door and down into the water.

"It's working!" Juliano yelled.

"Great!" Annie responded, but she was more interested in Alex's safety line. "Let's pull him back."

Juliano set a brake on the winch to slow down the rate of mooring cable payout and hopefully further slow down the propeller. Then he joined Annie on the second smaller winch to assist in winding back Alex's safety line.

On the bridge, the instruments were precisely registering the decline in speed that everybody was already noticing.

Merced and Ashton were hunched over a computer, shouting as if it were a video game.

"Twenty-three . . . twenty-two . . . twenty-one. . . ." Merced counted down the knots at which the ship was traveling.

"Come on, baby!" Ashton yelled at the computer.

"They're doing it!" Merced yelled in triumph. "We're slowing down."

That was evident too in the marina, at the back

of the ship. Geiger looked puzzled for a moment and keyed data into his handheld computer. He saw from the speed indicator that it had not been his imagination. The ship was indeed losing speed. He next called up a graphic of the ship on the screen and saw a warning light for an open loading dock door.

"No, you don't," he muttered, putting the computer away. From inside his bag he pulled a Glock pistol and cocked it. Then he walked purposefully back the way he'd come.

Beneath the ship, Alex had noticed a slight lessening in the power of the swirling currents of water as the ship slowed, but the currents remaining were powerful enough to create as many problems as he could handle. He felt a steady pull on his safety line, as Annie and Juliano winched it in. He checked his air, which was adequate, and allowed the line to pull him forward against the flow of water. The onrush of water was far too powerful for him to even try to swim against. All he could do was keep pointed in the right direction and allow himself to be pulled as a deadweight on the safety line.

But while Alex could endeavor to keep himself clear, he could not control his safety line forward of his position. At first he did not even see it become wound around the mooring line. His first inkling that something was wrong came with the sudden slackness on the safety line. He was being swept backward with the water flow. Thinking the safety line had snapped, he tried to swim clear of the ship. It was better to be left behind in one piece than in several, thanks to the propeller. That was when he found he was tethered to the mooring cable—and moving backward with it as it wound around the shaft of the giant screw.

Alex tried desperately to untie the safety line from around his waist, but he was already now in churning water near the back of the ship and he couldn't free himself as he was being tossed head over heels. He could even see the huge windmill blades sawing through the water—they hadn't been slowed as much as he'd hoped!

On the loading dock, Annie's eyes were wide with fear as she saw Alex's line now going out instead of coming in, as the small safety line winch was overcome by the winding power of the propeller. "We have to get him out of there!" she called to Juliano.

"Come on!" he said, bracing his foot against a bulwark. "Get some leverage!"

Together, they pulled on the safety line with all their might, but it continued to run through their hands, searing their palms. Their efforts were so wholehearted they failed to see Geiger, pistol in hand, directly behind them.

Geiger took in the scene quickly. Ignoring them, he watched the big winch paying out mooring cable and saw it as the source of the speed problem. Moving quickly to the winch and putting his pistol in his belt, he used both hands and the weight of his body to press down full on the brake to stop the winch. The brake clamped on the mooring cable and it stopped running over the side. The pulling power of the propeller was now set full against the holding power of the winch.

The propeller had slowed, but it was still being driven forcefully by the diesel engines. The winch shook, and the bolts in its base that held it to the metal deck began to loosen, the mooring cable stretching taut as a violin string. . . .

Beneath the ship, Alex was now less than twenty-five feet from the propeller. His only hope was to disentangle his safety line from the mooring cable. This he was doing with a lot of success, but he couldn't move fast enough to free its entire length before being drawn into the whirling blades.

Geiger moved back behind a big crate in the loading dock, still unseen by Annie and Juliano. He had his pistol ready, but right now he was more concerned with danger from the big winch. He wasn't sure he had done the right thing by clamping down the brake, but it was too late now to do anything about it. If that cable snapped, it could chop anyone in half that was near the winch. Geiger decided to stay out of harm's way for the moment and let events play themselves out. Then he would come in for the kill.

Meanwhile the cable stretched to near breaking point, and the winch with its bolts nearly lifted off the floor had struck fear into Annie and Juliano as well. They stared in fascination as the giant winch was slowly pulled from the steel deck like a recalcitrant carrot out of the ground. The winch seemed to hang on bitterly till the very end, and it appeared the mooring cable might go instead—its intertwined steel threads had been stretched visibly narrower. The winch base's last couple of bolts clung to the deck like roots in soil, until they popped simultaneously and whizzed out the open door like bullets. The big winch lifted a couple of feet in the air and fell on its side on the deck. Scraping across the deck in a shower of sparks, it headed for the door and the sea.

Annie and Juliano had to leap clear. He was a little less fast on his feet than her, and the base of the winch touched his arm—just barely—in what seemed like, at most, a gentle tap, before it disappeared over the side. It wasn't until Juliano tried to move, and ended up screaming and rolling in pain, that he discovered his shattered arm.

Alex saw it coming at him through the water—fast. He'd seen tanks charging through the scrub in Camp Pendleton. This looked like a Marineland version of that. This steel, squat, ugly piece of shit was coming through! This time it was going to be he who had to get out of its way.

In this split second, he recognized the hopelessness

of his position. Just behind his ass, he had a big propeller ready to slice him into cold cuts. In front of him, he had something that looked like a piece of the Santa Monica Pier exceeding the speed limit in the direction of his face. And he was attached by a steel cable at the bottom of a swiftly moving ship at sea. Not even Houdini had tried all this! Hell, not even Annie's previous cop boyfriend, whatever his name was . . .

Alex couldn't say what exactly happened. It was all too fast. The bow wave of what he now recognized as the winch seemed to push him out of the way, up toward the underside of the ship. He was left floating in the eighteen-inch space between the winch and the ship. As the mooring cable passed, it stripped itself loose of his safety line. After those two pieces of incredible good fortune, he couldn't complain about two pieces of bad luck. The winch had not followed the tapering side of the ship and hit the propeller. It had traveled in a straight line backward and missed the screw blades by what seemed to Alex like three or four inches. Then it seemed like the winch would anchor them where they were. But its weight, as it sank to the seabed, caused the mooring cable to unravel from around the prop, freeing it to revolve at full speed once more.

Next thing Alex felt was a strong pull on his safety line. The slack had been picked up and he was now, once again, being hauled forward deadweight against the water flow. With a smile on his face, he visualized Annie at the winch. She wasn't going to give him too much leash. Above him, he saw a dark rectangle that would be the door of the loading dock, and he broke the surface directly beneath it. Annie smiled and waved and then turned off the safety line winch.

Treading water at the end of a short length of safety line, Alex turned off his air and raised his mask. Annie looked fine, but he saw that Juliano, on his feet again, was nursing what looked like a broken arm. "What happened?" he asked Annie as she bent over the edge to help him out of the water.

As she was pulling Alex, Annie suddenly felt the cold barrel of a gun pressed against the back of her neck. "Let him go," Geiger ordered her, in a cold, gloating voice.

Alex had not seen him in time to warn her. Juliano looked on helplessly. Annie did not want to obey, but Alex answered Geiger by pulling his hand out of her grasp. He was left sitting on the lip of the open doorway, his feet dangling above the water.

Geiger watched Alex carefully for a few moments, and then appeared to relax as he felt in control. He turned to Annie and said unhurriedly, "I don't think your boyfriend appreciates the logistics involved in ramming the most automated ship in the world into a fully loaded fuel tanker with no set anchor pattern."

"Probably not," Annie agreed, humoring him.

Then Geiger turned to Alex, challenging once

more. "You slowed it down," he said, "but you're not going to stop it!" He caught Annie by one arm.

"Let her go," Alex said.

Geiger pulled Annie closer to him and put the pistol barrel to her temple.

Alex said soothingly. "Go and live the rest of your days on some island, sticking leeches on your ass."

"So you met my nurses?" Geiger grinned. "They clean the copper out of my blood. Doctors give me three to six months to live. Those bloodsuckers might give me a few more."

"You'll have a lot less than that if you don't let Annie go."

In a sudden rage, Geiger turned the pistol on Alex, who quickly pushed off the lip of the doorway into the water.

Alex surfaced once more, ready to dive instantly if Geiger decided to shoot. He saw that Geiger had stepped back and was covering Annie with the gun once more. Maintaining an upright position in the fast-moving water at the end of a short length of safety line, he noticed that his air line was hanging free. Touching his hand to his head, he realized that his mask was gone. Diving in to escape the gunshot had knocked it off its resting place on his head and it had been swept away.

Geiger was standing near the safety line winch. Without warning, he put his left hand out and released the line. Alex barely had time to fill his lungs with air before being sucked underwater and

carried beneath the ship on his way back to the propeller, which was revolving at full speed once more.

On the loading dock, Geiger watched, in satisfaction, Annie's dismay at Alex's disappearance
beneath the surface. He turned to the ship's officer
with the broken arm and saw fear on the man's face.
"I hope you don't mind, Mr. Juliano," Geiger said.
"Annie's coming with me as a little extra insurance."

Geiger advanced on him quickly. Catching him
off balance, he had no difficulty pushing Juliano
through the doorway and into the sea. "You know
the one-armed freestyle, don't you?" Geiger called
after him.

But Juliano was already beneath the surface and
missed the joke.

"Come on, Annie!" Geiger said, trying to pull her
with him.

"No!" she screamed, holding on to the safety line
winch.

"You want to join them?" he asked threateningly.

"Yes!"

Geiger ignored that and continued to pull her. At
last, he broke her hold on the safety winch, but she
struggled with him all the way off the loading dock
and quieted down only when they were deeper
inside the ship. She glanced back once at the winch
to make sure that the rewind button she'd managed
to press was doing its job. The safety line was taut
and coming in again. Having seen that, she distracted Geiger with some fresh antics.

Beneath the surface, Juliano kept his eyes open. As he sank, he managed to use his good hand to grab onto the safety line. But he could not prevent the line from running through his hand, and he was swept backward along it until he bumped into Alex. Without his mask, Alex was having big problems himself. All the same, he clutched Juliano tightly and tried to hold his breath until the safety line hauled them to the surface.

All his instincts told him to breathe in, *now*. His muscles needed oxygen, and they sent chemical messengers through his bloodstream to his brain, saying, in their own wordless ways, *Air, air*! Those parts of his body that his mind did not control—the nervous system that caused his lungs to expand and his heart to beat without any thought on his part—were growing rebellious. Soon they would overthrow his mind, open his mouth and have him breathe in. But Alex was a cop, and this wasn't the first time he'd ever had to hold his breath in an emergency. He knew he could do it. His brain told his rebellious body parts not to cross the line. He held his breath, even though his eyeballs felt like they were popping, stars floated across his eyes that he knew were not air bubbles, he felt dizzy, he felt pain . . .

Juliano was not able to hold out. His body convulsed as he breathed in the saltwater and began to drown. His grip weakened on the safety line and his hand fell away, only to sink its fingers into Alex's shirt. Alex held him. Otherwise he was gone.

Breaking the surface, Alex gasped like a sea lion. He heaved Juliano's twitching body up on the lip of the loading dock doorway and climbed up himself. Having switched off the winch and kicked off his flippers, he lay Juliano on his belly and pumped water from his lungs. The officer came to right away, stimulated by the pain in his broken arm. Alex got him to his feet. There was no time to get him a painkiller.

"Which way did they go?" Alex asked.

Still spitting and trickling seawater, Juliano said, "Toward the marina. He's jumping ship."

. . . . .

The captain arrived on the bridge of the super-tanker in his robe. When a bridge officer had woken him in his cabin by phone, he'd cursed out the man as someone who could not handle respon-sibility. If the officer wanted to make a career for himself, he would have to learn to take care of problems on his own, without always looking for approval from higher authority. The officer politely agreed with the ship's master, but thought, all the same, he should come to the bridge as fast as his feet could carry him. Now the captain trained his binoculars through a bridge window on a large white vessel not far away and approaching fast. He looked into the prow of the ship. It was heading right for them! The captain then looked at the radar screen, as if doubting what his eyes had seen.

"She's closing at eighteen knots," the officer told him, "bearing two-one-five straight into us."

"I can't get them on the radio, Captain," another officer said. "She's not responding."

The captain took another quick look through his binoculars, let them swing from their strap around his neck and shook bewilderment and sleep from his head. "Get the anchors up, now!" he said.

Geiger pushed Annie in front of him. She stumbled and tried to delay him, almost pushing him to the point of shooting her several times. He was losing his patience with this pair. As he'd anticipated, no

one else aboard had offered him anything that
could be called resistance. Then along came this
hyperactive L.A. cop and his flaky girlfriend. In all
his cruises, he had never seen anything like this
pair! At the beginning, he'd thought they might
add a little spice to the otherwise boring menu he
had planned. That would have been all right. It
could even have been fun . . . But not when they
started seriously messing with his plans in ways he
hadn't foreseen. That was too much to tolerate.

Now that one-half of the relationship had been
sent to Davy Jones's locker, he'd been prepared to be
more lenient with the girl. So long as she was coop-
erative with him in all ways, of course. He wasn't
going to waste his time on a woman who did not
know how to enjoy herself. He had no time left to
waste. It would be up to her. . . . This was why he
hadn't shot her yet, though he was sorely tempted to.

They walked into the marina. With a few keyboard commands on his handheld computer,
Geiger set the ship's huge retractable marina doors
in opening motion. He got a charge out of that—
opening massive steel structures that weighed hundreds of tons with a gadget that weighed five
ounces. These were the biggest automatic garage
doors in the world!

Pushing Annie ahead of him and keeping her
covered with the pistol, Geiger went down into the
well of the marina, where windsurfers, sailfish, jet
skis, small sailboats and speedboats were parked

neatly in rows. The craft were ready to be pushed into the water through the doors, which opened at sea level, letting the well fill to a few inches to ease the launching of the craft.

He headed for a Wind-Jet 44, in the front row next to the doors. This craft was really two side-by-side jet skis joined by a removable section.

Geiger motioned for Annie to sit on one of the joined jet skis. "This time you get a window seat," he said. Then, still holding the pistol in his left hand, with a length of mooring rope he used his right hand to expertly tie her wrists together  and then to the front of the jet ski.

The big marina doors were still in the process of opening as Geiger pushed the craft into the water. The doors had by now parted wide enough for the craft to fit through and make for the open water. He started the engine on his side, and then on hers. Having adjusted the controls so that he alone managed the craft, Geiger sat on his jet ski and eased the Wind-Jet 44 through the open doors.

"You better hang on," he yelled to Annie, as if she had any choice, and accelerated hard.


Alex reached the back of the ship, on the deck above the marina, as the Wind-Jet passed through the opening doors. In a wild leap from the deck rail, he landed on top of one door, lost his balance, fell and clung to it by one hand.

"Annie . . . no!" he shouted down to her.

Looking up, she saw him dangling from the marina door and desperately tried to free her wrists. She couldn't.

The Wind-Jet bounced around on the churning water in the wake of the ship. The marina doors were designed to be used when the vessel was at rest. The light craft were never meant to navigate the turbulence behind a moving ship. The Wind-Jet bucked like a horse taken in from new grass. Geiger barely hung on to the controls. Annie was nearly unseated and dragged by her wrists. She only just managed to stay on her jet ski until the craft reached less turbulent water and sped away from the *Seabourn Legend*.

Trying to pull himself up on the door, Alex slipped and nearly fell backward into the roiling wake of the ship. Had he fallen, he would have been left with a long swim in front of him, after a long hard night and a difficult morning. He hung on.

When he looked up, he saw Dante on the deck that he'd jumped from above the marina. Only the photographer was making no effort to help him . . . he was taking photos of him!

Alex gave him a real dirty look.

"Jesus, man," Dante shouted after lowering his camera, "I think I just won the Pulitzer prize."

His doubled camera strap hung over the deck rail, not far above Alex's head. "Give me your camera strap!" Alex yelled.

For a moment Dante looked as if he would not do anything to endanger his camera. Then he thought better of it and lowered the doubled strap within reach of Alex. With the strap in one hand, and Dante pulling with both hands at the other end of it, Alex climbed to the top of the door and then to the deck above.

Easing over the deck rail, Alex asked, "You know your way around the ship?"

"Yeah," Dante acknowledged.

"Then come on!"

Passengers huddled around the windows of the sky deck, looking out at the supertanker. Some were just beginning to have serious doubts.

"I think we're coming in a little fast," Frank remarked.

Others, like Isabel, knew instinctively that they were headed for trouble. Her husband, Alejandro, tried to comfort her. Sobbing, she said to him, "How can this happen on our honeymoon?"

Liza, the entertainment director, was determined to fulfill her professional responsibilities. There was nothing in her training that helped her deal with a supertanker, but she knew all about St. Martin and decided to concentrate on that instead. "Listen up, folks," she said in her distinctive, far-carrying voice, "we are nearing one of the G-spots of the Caribbean. Great beaches. Great shopping. Great night life.

Saint Martin, we call it in English. One part of the island is French, and the other part Dutch. The French pronounce it *Sanh Martanh*, and the Dutch say *Sint Maarten*. It's one of the Dutch Windward Islands, which is part of the Netherland Antilles. Of course, the French regard it as part of the French West Indies and as the westernmost part of France itself. I hope all that's clear."

"I don't think we will ever live to see this crazy island," Isabel said in a petrified voice.

Liza took a deep breath and went on before anyone could stop her: "On his second voyage, Columbus discovered this island on Saint Martin's Day, but of course he called it San Martino. Anyway, the French and Dutch solved their argument about who should have what by getting a wine-drinking Frenchman and a gin-drinking Dutchman to walk around the island to see how much territory each could cover and claim for his country. The Frenchman outwalked the Dutchman and got more territory for France, but the Dutchman headed for the best territory and claimed that for Holland . . ."

Knowing that Liza was unstoppable, Debbie and Harvey worked around her, ushering passengers away from the windows.

"We have to get back as far as we can," Harvey told people.

Drew and her parents immediately followed his advice.

"Could we use life jackets as padding?" Rupert wondered.

"Stay away from any glass," Debbie said.

"What did she say about Columbus?" Isabel wanted to know, a bit irritated by the penetrating quality of Liza's voice.

"Nothing bad," Alejandro assured her.

"I wish he were here now," she said. "Columbus would know how not to bump into a huge ship."

Sheri, the band leader, was immersed in her own private trouble. She depended on her agent for work, and in return paid him a generous commission on her earnings. This cruise had been his idea. Totally. It would never have crossed her mind. He had sent her here. What she needed to think about now was, what kind of agent would risk her career like this? She worked hard. People liked her music. Was this to be her reward? What was on his mind to do this to her? What had she done to him? Her commissions had put at least two of his kids through college. Partway, at least. This was what she got in the way of gratitude! Dangerous work in a combat zone! She made up her mind, already feeling better, and voiced her resolution aloud: "My agent is so fired."

Isabel burst into tears. Alejandro tried to comfort her, but she was inconsolable. "We had such a short, happy life together," she sobbed.

. . .

Pleased with his getaway from the cruise ship and with how his plan was working out, Geiger was in a sunny mood. He wanted Annie to appreciate him, to know that now she was with a man of superior ability.

Glancing back at the *Seabourn Legend*, he shouted across to her, above the engine noise and slapping of water, "When the autopilot on that ship rams her into a ten-million-dollar supertanker, I have a feeling my computer program won't be so popular."

Annie was defiant. "They'll stop it!" she shouted back.

He said with a thin smile, "I don't think you want to be on that ship right now."

People weren't happy to be on the supertanker either. The entire tanker crew was up and mobilizing, but chaos and sheer pandemonium had the upper hand.

On the supertanker bridge, the captain asked, "How long before we have power?"

"Seven, eight minutes, sir," an officer answered.

"In eight minutes we'll be blown out of the water!" the captain declared. "Hurry, dammit!"


Alex and Dante rushed through the casino—the entire ship looked like a war zone—and made their way into the atrium, which was completely engulfed in flames.

Dante was having second thoughts about helping Alex. "Where are we going?" he asked nervously.

"The bow thrusters," Alex answered. "You know a shortcut?"

Dante pointed to the leaping flames. "It's that way," he said. "We can't go through there."

Looking around them, Alex saw that the fire raged across the side exits and also blocked a flight of stairs, effectively sealing one part of the ship from the other. His eye caught something behind him, in the casino, a Ducati 916 motorcycle on a pedestal above a row of slot machines. He wondered if it had gas in the tank. There was only one way to find out. Getting Dante to stand with him on the bench holding the slot machines, Alex used his help in lifting the bike off the pedestal, first onto the bench and then onto the floor.

Alex stood astride the Ducati and kick-started it. The engine roared to life. He looked at Dante and pointed to the pillion seat.

Looking even more anxious than before, the photographer climbed on.

"Hang on!" Alex warned him.

"I'm right behind you," Dante assured him.

## 16

Juliano limped onto the bridge, clutching his useless arm. Merced and Ashton helped him to a chair. After a moment of looking out a window at the nearing supertanker—he no longer needed binoculars for this!—Juliano grabbed the radio transmitter in his good hand and switched on the ship's public address system.

"Alex, can you hear me?" he asked. "If you can hear me, use the ship's intercom. We're running out of time."

In the casino, Alex spotted an intercom on the wall behind the slot machines. He eased off the motorbike throttle to cut engine noise and said into the intercom, "I can't talk right now."

He gunned the Ducati engine. The bike did a wheelie as it took off out of the casino and into the burning atrium, Alex going for maximum acceleration in the shortest possible distance as he headed straight for a wall of thick smoke and bright orange flames. What he hadn't seen or remembered were six steps leading down from the casino level to the atrium floor. By the time he did see them, it was too late and he had no choice but to go airborne. The bike rose in an arc from the top step and went so high that Alex had to duck, and Dante hit his head against the bottom of the chandelier.

The Ducati went through the fire in midair, like a circus tiger jumping through a flaming hoop, except this was no hoop. The whole atrium was blazing. For a few seconds they saw nothing all around but the leaping flames—and then the bike came down hard, with fire all around them. The bike almost spun out, but Alex fought it and managed to steady it. He saw a way out of the inferno down a spiral staircase and he bounced the bike down the corkscrew steps.

"I'm on fire!" Dante screamed.

"This will kill it!" Alex shouted back, just before he slammed through a large glass door, shattering it into a million pieces.

On the other side of the door, down a flight of steps, the corridor was filled with water. The bike landed with a huge splash and its engine promptly died. Alex and Dante sat on the bike in shock, in water up to their waists. But at least Dante's clothes had stopped burning. He looked at some still smoldering places, while Alex reached out to an intercom on the wall beside them.

"Juliano, this is Alex," he said. "I'm going after the bow thrusters."

Juliano looked out the bridge window. The supertanker was now less than two miles away. "You flooded it," he said. "There's no way to get there."

"I'll get there," Alex told him. "Talk me through."

"The bow thrusters are two large wheels connected by a small shaft," Juliano said. He wiped the sweat from his eyes. His broken arm was now bleeding. Gritting his teeth against the pain, he went on, "You can find them at the end of the shaft that runs below the bilge pump room."

The Wind-Jet skimmed over the waves. Geiger was euphoric. Things were going his way, all the way! He had a bag of diamonds. The cruise ship—the pride and joy of his ungrateful ex-employers—was about to hit a loaded oil tanker. And he'd outsmarted the dumb cop and stolen his girlfriend. There were a lot of people out there now who wished they hadn't messed with him. He'd shown them. They'd never forget him. He was in control. This was his show. He was enjoying himself!

It disgusted Annie to see Geiger chortling to

himself in smug self-satisfaction and triumph. Even
if something terrible happened to the ship . . . Even
if something terrible happened to Alex . . . She
couldn't bring herself to think about this possibility.
No matter what happened, she would find a way to
make Geiger suffer for what he'd done and was doing
to them all. He would regret it. She would see to that.

How she would go about making him sorry, she
didn't know yet. But she had one great advantage
over Geiger. He underestimated her. When she did
something, it would take him by surprise. If only
she could think of something. . . . Annie went on
trying to loosen the bonds on her wrists. Looking
down, she noticed a warning label on the connect-
ing piece between the two jet skis. In spite of the
motion and bouncing, she read: WARNING! DO NOT
DISENGAGE WHILE MOVING. That was food for
thought, she decided.

Heading for a small island that lay off the big
island of St. Martin, Geiger smiled to himself and
tossed his handheld computer over his shoulder
into the bright blue water.

Alex got off the bike and waded through the
waist-deep water in the corridor. He had to turn
back to motion Dante to follow him. The photographer seemed reluctant to leave the pillion seat.
He finally did, and the bike fell on its side
beneath the water.

Soon the corridor water was chest deep and Alex found it easier to swim. Dante didn't like this at all. But what could he do? Behind him was fire, and in front of him water. He had a choice—he could drown or be roasted to death. He swam. Dante was beginning to feel a bit better about things, until he saw two large fish swim by him. There was worse to come. Alex had found a sign that read: BILGE PUMP ROOM. The bad news was that the sign had a downward-pointing arrow. They were already up to their armpits in water. There was no way he was going down lower in the ship! Dante resolved.

Alex pointed down and, without waiting for a response, took a breath and dived beneath the surface.

Dante saw him disappear down a submerged stairwell. "This is crazy," he complained out loud. But not wanting to die alone, he took a deep breath and followed Alex.

The corridor at the foot of the stairs was filled to its ceiling with water, but the ship's lighting system had so far survived, despite being submerged. Dante met Alex swimming back into the corridor out of a room and shaking his head. He pointed to a hatchway farther along and they swam there. Inside the hatchway was a large room—with about a foot of air between the water and ceiling. They popped their heads up into that space and gasped in air for some moments before speaking.

"Where are we?" Alex asked.

"I don't know," Dante admitted.

They heard Juliano's voice over a distant intercom, somewhere above water level. The acoustics of the compressed space made the senior officer's voice sound like a cartoon character's or as if he'd been breathing helium.

"You only turn one wheel at a time," Juliano instructed. "If you turn them both, you're canceling yourself out. Make sure you turn the starboard wheel."

Alex looked a bit confused.

Dante faced toward the front of the ship and held up his right hand. "This is starboard," he said.

"Follow me," Alex said, and took a deep breath.

Dante swam underwater after him. The lights everywhere made it feel like an aquarium. But Dante didn't like the feeling of being a fish.

They located the shaft beneath the bilge pump room and followed it until they saw the two bow thrusters at the front of the ship. Then they had to find themselves some air in a hurry. They were lucky. Not far away, the water in one area was only shoulder deep. They stood there breathing and resting, though knowing all the while that every second counted now.

From the windows of the sky deck, where Harvey and Debbie sat in their underwear holding each other, the side of the supertanker filled the sky.

"Remember how big we thought the *Seabourn*

*Legend* was when we first saw it?" Harvey said. "Look at this sucker!"

"I'm scared!" Debbie whined, clutching him.

"Relax!" Harvey said and jutted out his lower jaw. "You're with me. You don't have a thing to worry about."

"Oh, Harvey, I'm sorry for being mean to you."

"You weren't mean, honey bunch."

"Oh, yes, I was, Harvey."

"Well," Harvey said, reconsidering, "you made me take off my pants."

"We were smothering from the smoke," Debbie pointed out.

"I didn't want to take off my pants," Harvey said, getting argumentative.

Debbie glanced out the window at the supertanker's looming wall of steel. "I'm sorry, Harvey," she piped in a little girl's voice.

He patted her hand and kissed her cheek.


Alex and Dante swam back once more to the wheel of the starboard bow thruster. They had already made two trips and returned for air. By now they had their act down and were getting the wheel to move. But they had much less leverage working underwater, and it needed all their strength, working together, even to get the wheel to budge. They then both combined their force until one or the other had to give in, and they both returned for air.

"Do you think it's working?" Alex asked when they were once more in their breathing space.

Dante was too far gone to reply just yet.

"Have you noticed any change in the ship's direction?" Alex asked again.

Dante hit his right forehead and water poured out of his left ear. "Alex, I'm down here in the sea with goddamn fish! Why are you asking me?"

Alex laughed. "You ever thought about becoming a cop, Dante?" he asked.

Dante saw nothing funny in that. He looked around the water-filled interior and said very seriously, "I never thought this is how I would die."

"Once more?" Alex asked, pointing into the water.

Dante nodded.

On the bridge, Merced excitedly rapped the compass on its side to make it move faster. "They're turning us!" he said.

Juliano, slumped in his chair in pain and exhaustion, looked out the window. "It's too late," he said.

"The tanker is moving too!" Merced said, still trying to believe a collision could be avoided.

It was true. The oil tanker's anchors were pulled above the waterline and were now slowly swinging free on lengths of chain from the prow. Juliano shook his head. Too little, too late.

On the tanker's bridge the captain stared out at the cruise ship run amok. His anchors were up, his port engines full steam ahead, his starboard engines full steam astern. . . . He was trying to turn this big baby where she sat in the water. His crew had done what they could, and he had nothing against them now for hiding themselves in safe places—if they could find any. As captain, he would stay on the bridge. There was nothing more for him to do either.

The tanker was turning, its giant bulk beginning to stir, like a hibernating bear in early spring. As a Norwegian champion kayaker, and as a seaman who had served on a fast and maneuverable destroyer in his country's navy, the captain had only tolerant amusement for the handling capabilities of this big ship. It took a long time to get moving, and once it was moving, it took even longer to stop. He liked to say to other master mariners that navigating a supertanker was a lot like driving an overloaded semi-trailer at well over the speed limit on a crowded highway. Just don't anyone get nervous and make a mistake.

With an expressionless face he looked out at the big cruise ship bearing down on him. It was veering away from him at the last minute! Apparently the madman at its controls was chickening out. Or maybe he was such a poor seaman, he thought this was only going to be a near miss. The sea had taught the captain to accept the power of forces greater than his own. Now he had to accept being rammed by a luxury cruise ship. A torpedo from a nuclear submarine would have been an honorable way to go. . . . Please God, not a cruise ship!

The tanker's prow turned some more away from the approaching ship. And the cruise ship veered some more to avoid collision. It wouldn't ram the tanker full on, but neither ship had changed course enough or in time to avoid a collision. The captain shook his head slowly from side to side.

On the sky deck there was silence except for occasional sobs and prayers. Everyone had pulled back far enough to avoid being thrown overboard or hit by flying glass. Drew sat between her parents. Each held a hand. She looked from one to the other. Then she freed her hands.

"I know Mom is scared," Drew signed. "Are you scared, Dad?"

Rupert nodded.

"That's all right, Dad," Drew signed. She consoled him by squeezing his hand. "I am, too."

"We're in God's hands," Celeste signed. "His will be done."

"Amen," Rupert signed.

"I'm sorry about wearing that dress," Drew signed.

All three looked at the oily, raggedy remains of her dress and burst out laughing.

A second later the *Seabourn Legend*'s prow scraped along the supertanker's side.

The passengers on the sky deck watched in a dread, fascinated near silence, as it seemed, for a little while, that their ship might or might not graze by the oil tanker without touching it. When they saw that they were going to hit it, still no one screamed or shouted. With a rending sound of steel on steel, the front of the *Seabourn Legend* sideswiped the oil tanker. Then passengers screamed as they were thrown from their places of refuge, clutching their loved ones. They sprawled and tumbled as the deck heaved and pitched.

The *Seabourn Legend* ran its nose along the side of the tanker, with loud grinding and crunching noises. Fountains of sparks rose in the air. But the cruise ship was like a bull calf butting its head into the unyielding side of the herd's dominant animal. The supertanker gave a small shrug of annoyance but stayed put. The prow of the cruise ship crumpled like paper.

The smaller ship's nose continued to grind along the front side of the tanker, scraping paint away. Gradually the two ships came almost side by side, facing the same way. As the *Seabourn Legend* passed the stationary tanker, people could look through the portholes from one ship into the other. Despite their disparity in size, the captain's bridge was almost on the same level in both ships. The tanker captain's expressionless seadog gaze cut like a laser beam into the bridge of the passing cruise ship. But all the tanker captain saw were the faces of Juliano, Merced, and Ashton frozen in shock. After they passed, this encounter was still as much of a mystery to him as ever.

The captain had more important worries than physical damage to his tanker. The first of these was fear of a breach in the oil-containing holds and a consequent oil spill in this picturesque part of the Caribbean. The other big worry was fire. Every man coming aboard the tanker was searched for cigarettes and matches or a lighter, and on board everyone wore runner-soled shoes. The deckhands' everyday chipping and maintenance work was always suspended when the ship was loaded with oil. The fumes around the ship were often so dense,

it was hard to breathe. Some people said that sunlight magnified by or reflected from a shiny surface
was enough to ignite a whole ship.

The captain saw his worst fears come true. The
shock of the impact ruptured some pipes on the
tanker's foredeck, spilling oil in a spreading pool.
The sparks from the friction of steel plates set this
pool ablaze. He pressed on the fire alarms and acti-
vated automated firefighting systems. These
spewed foam to a depth of several feet over the oil,
quenching the flames. But black smoke rising
through the foam signified that there was still oil
burning underneath. The emergency fire crews
turned stopcocks to cut off the supply of oil to that
section of piping, and extinguished the flames completely.

The captain breathed a sigh of relief. If this
tanker had blown, they might have found pieces of
it and the cruise ship as far away as Florida.


Alex and Dante had only just surfaced for a breath
of air when the *Seabourn Legend*'s prow hit the
tanker. They stood in the compartment near the
bow thrusters where the water was shoulder deep.
The impact knocked them off their feet and water
surged into the compartment up to the ceiling.
They were tossed around like goldfish in a bowl,
but the dense seawater prevented them from being
thrown too hard against the metal walls, floor, or

ceiling. After the initial surge, the water almost drained completely from the compartment, as the ship rebounded from the impact. Alex and Dante were left sitting in a few inches of water in the middle of the floor. They breathed in and out deeply while they could—waiting for the water to surge in again and cover them completely. It did. But after that they were able to keep their heads above the water.

The part of the prow that crumpled was several levels above and forward of where they were. All the damage was above water level and would not be a problem in calm seas. But neither man knew any of that.

Dante cocked his head to one side. "Hey, we're not sinking," he pronounced.

Alex had no idea how he knew that. Perhaps they would have hit the bottom by now.

Dante grinned and slapped Alex on the shoulder. "We turned her!" he shouted. "We really did!"

Alex nodded. He had to allow that they were not on the bottom of the sea, they were not being deep-fried in boiling oil. . . . It seemed like the same old cruise again—the noise, the filth, the hard labor and high risk. He was almost used to it by now. He was about to say so when he noticed something that took the words out of his mouth.

The steel plates in the side of the ship next to where they stood had begun to bulge inward like soggy newspaper.

•       •       •

Frank thought that his wife was dead. She lay pale and motionless on the sky deck, and her head was slightly askew, as if her neck was broken. He sank to his knees beside her body.

"Constance, my dear," he said in a pleading voice, wringing his hands, "please, please, be all right. If you have passed on, I cannot go on living without you." He looked down at her lifeless face and closed eyelids. "If only you were restored to me once more in health, I would never say a word to you against smoking cigarettes."

Her eyes opened. "You wouldn't?" she asked.

"Constance, darling, you're alive!" Frank said with delight. "Shall I try to find you a cigarette?"

She sat up and straightened her hair. Frank helped her to her feet. "What were you saying?" she asked.

"About a cigarette."

"I thought you promised never to mention them again," she said.

"No, no—" He stopped to think. "Really?"

"I gave them up, Frank," she said firmly. "But if you were to find an unopened bottle of champagne rolling about somewhere in this shipwreck, I would not refuse some—if you can also find a clean glass."

"Yes, dear," Frank said.

•       •       •

On the bridge, Merced held onto the nonfunctioning wheel as the prow of the *Seabourn Legend* finally scraped along as far as the prow of the tanker and passed it. Both ships now became free of one another. He gave the useless wheel a spin and whispered hoarsely, "When I was nine, I went downhill on my new bicycle and saw the wall coming and couldn't avoid it." He was near tears.

Juliano was slumped in his chair and seemed about to lose consciousness. Ashton took notice of this. Now that the immediate threat to his own had lifted, at least for the moment, the welfare of the senior officer became uppermost in his mind. He went to the first aid locker and filled a syringe with painkiller. After he'd injected it in Juliano's good arm, he waited a minute for it to take effect before examining the other arm. At least one forearm bone was broken, possibly both.

"Mr. Merced," Ashton said, "give me a hand with a splint and bandages. We'll have you more comfortable in no time, sir."

"Thank you," Juliano murmured. Then he became more alert and asked suspiciously, "Do you know what that Los Angeles cop is up to now?"

On the sky deck the sisters Fran and Ruby suddenly changed from painfully shy, socially awkward single women who were no longer young, into practical, nononsense administrators of help to those in need.

They methodically went from passenger to passenger, making sure that no one was hurt or disoriented.

"Your daughter," Fran said, when they came to Drew and her parents. "Tell her we want to know whether she has hurt herself."

"She's all right," Celeste said.

Fran was polite but firm. "Just do this for me, dear," she said. "Ask her."

Celeste began signing and talking simultaneously. "They want to know if you—"

Drew had read their lips and gave them a thumbs-up sign and a smile.

"I hope you don't mind me remarking," Rupert began diplomatically, "on how you two have come out of your shells to help everyone in this disaster."

"This is nothing," Fran said dismissively. "Now, a grass fire on the prairie, that's something."

"Or tornadoes," Ruby added.

"Them, certainly," Fran agreed. "Though I reckon a three-day blizzard is worst."

"Especially if you don't know where the stock is and you got to go find them," Ruby said. "Them critters die of thirst out there in the snow. They don't know it's made of water."

Drew began giggling and got a sharp nudge from her mother.


The Wind-Jet had traveled nearly a mile across the calm blue waters toward the small island off

St. Martin. A smile of self-gratification was pasted on Geiger's face as he steered the craft. Annie's wrists were still bound to the front of her jet ski.

Looking back, she saw the *Seabourn Legend* pass the supertanker. From her fairly distant viewpoint, it looked as if there had been no collision. She'd been certain there would be. "They missed!" she shouted triumphantly to Geiger over the engine noise.

He looked back for a few seconds and then faced her. "Impossible," he said, plainly not believing his eyes. He looked back again, as if this time it would be different. But there it was, plain to see—the cruise ship was steaming away from the oil tanker. "*Impossible!*" Geiger screamed in an unearthly howl. He looked at Annie once more. This time his face was twisted like a gargoyle's.

She found all the fear, loathing, disgust, and anger he felt for his fellow human beings focused and concentrated on her.

Liza, the entertainment director, had done what she saw as her best to distract passengers before the two ships collided. Distracting passengers and making them forget their worries were part of her job description. As a professional, she took her duties seriously. As the two ships neared one another and she failed to get positive feedback from the passengers, it all became too much for her. Liza's eyes glazed over and she slowly became transfixed. Her loud voice no longer reverberated on the sky deck.

With the danger past, Liza, like someone perfectly preserved emerging slowly from a melting glacier, was finding her voice again—and her dedication to her duties. Those nearest her were startled when she suddenly addressed the passengers on the deck in a ringing voice.

"On Saint Martin, you'll find lots of duty-free shops in the Dutch capital of Philipsburg," she told them, "mostly along Front Street. But it can get pretty crowded, especially if other cruise ships are in town. Let me give you one of Liza's Shopping Tips . . ." She looked brightly around. "I always make the trip across the island to the French capital of Marigot—there's no problem with border crossings or passports and it's much less crowded. You can buy quality items like French perfume there at a quarter the price you can at home."

Sheri said to her in a low voice, "If I pushed you overboard, people would think it was an accident. No one here would turn me in."

In front of his eyes, Alex saw the wall of the ship start to buckle inward into the compartment in which he and Dante stood, shoulder deep in seawater.

"Get down!" Alex yelled and pulled Dante with him beneath the surface of the water. They swam underwater to the back wall of the compartment and surfaced. The two men did not know it, but this was the moment when the two ships were sliding past one another, prow-to-prow. What they saw was a massive pointed piece of steel pierce the side of the ship. It poked its way inward, and Dante recognized it.

"The bill!" he said, his eyes wide. "And now the fluke!"

"It's a goddamn anchor!" Alex said.

One arm of the supertanker's nearest anchor, dangling from its prow, had snagged the moving cruise ship. Like a tree thorn caught in the sleeve of a passerby, it ripped the fabric of the ship. As the *Seabourn Legend* went forward, the anchor arm pulled tight against the steel plates of the ship's side, which were eight feet high and twelve feet long. Rivets popped and ricocheted off the compartment walls like jumbo-sized bullets. The plates fell off the ship like playing cards. Then the anchor ripped free.

Alex and Dante had to cling to the wall behind them to avoid being swept out through the hole as the water drained from the ship.

"Oh, shit!" Alex said.

Dante looked across at him. " 'Oh shit what?' " he wanted to know, guessing that maybe their troubles weren't over. He saw Alex looking out the hole in the ship's side. Dante looked in that direction.

The hole was located where the ship's side

narrowed inward to the prow. Thus it provided a more or less forward view.

A big harbor lay dead ahead of the ship, about half a mile away. Judging by the speed with which the water seemed to be going by, Alex figured they had come back close to full steam ahead.

Although it was still early morning in Philipsburg, quite a few locals and tourists were in the streets. The town stretched about a mile along the shore of Great Bay and consisted of three more or less parallel streets: Front Street (Voorstraat in Dutch), Back Street, and Pondfill. All the buildings in Front and Back streets, in various pastel shades with gingerbread trims, seemed to be duty-free stores, hotels, casinos, or restaurants. Narrow alleys led to courtyards with climbing flowers on the walls.

While it never got as hot and humid here as on other islands, people were in the habit of going about their business early to avoid the full power of the midday sun. Avid shoppers were scurrying from store to store, some already heavily loaded down with bags at this early hour. Others, who had spent the previous night until the early morning hours at nightclubs and casinos, were having small breakfasts and large coffees at tables outside cafés. As they sat, the sun, the good humor of the people, and the beauty of the scene helped their recoveries get started. A few were already ordering drinks.

The outdoors crowd was headed for the harbor, or already there. A pier ran out into the bay, on which people were walking and jogging. In the harbor, hundreds of craft of all kinds rode at anchor or were moored at marinas. Seagoing trawlers, small off-island fishing boats, and oarlocked work boats were mixed with luxury yachts, sleek deepwater sailboats with towering masts, small sailboats, and little pleasure craft of every description, all the way down to air-filled rubber rafts.

Fishermen washed down the decks of their boats, and one walked from the docks toward town, dragging in each hand along the ground behind him a huge billfish. While the fishermen worked on their boats silently and expertly, the visitors getting their sailboats ready to go out shouted frequent nautical commands to one another. One man managed to fall overboard while the sailboat was still at anchor, and on several other boats loud misunderstandings and even emergencies were occurring.

This was just another sunny morning on this

island paradise. People were engrossed in their own occupations or pastimes. No one paid any attention to the big white ship steaming across the bay toward the harbor. It was just another cruise ship. . . .

Alex had no wish to swim back through corridors and up stairwells to see how the fire in the atrium was progressing. He needed to find an alternative route to the upper decks. He saw a solution at the edge of the gaping hole in the side of the ship, gouged by the oil tanker's anchor. A rope ladder thrown over the side for the ship's evacuation was swinging within his grasp. He and Dante could climb up it, but they needed to hurry. Alex didn't want to be down at the lower front part of the ship, if it decided to take on the island. He knew who was going to win. And it wasn't going to be the *Seabourn Legend*.

He caught hold of the rope ladder and beckoned to Dante. The photographer shook his head. "Come on!" Alex said. "Hurry!"

"Will it hold?" Dante asked.

Alex pulled hard on the ladder by way of an answer. It held firm.

"You go first," Dante said.

Alex swung out onto the ladder and began climbing. "Come on!" he shouted down.

The photographer stuck his head out the hole

like a nervous gopher. He took forever to get on the ladder and kept looking up to see if there was any sign of it giving way. Alex recognized that he'd pushed the man to his limit. Dante had been brave and helpful up this point, but he could not go much further. Instead of cussing him out, Alex was uncharacteristically patient and silent.

Dante finally got both hands and both feet on the rope ladder. Knowing enough to avoid looking down at the swirling water beneath him, he onerously climbed rung by rung, like a sleepy squirrel.

The cruise ship was beginning to cut through crowded waters. Most of the boats scooted out of the way in plenty of time. But one skipper of a thirty-six-foot deepwater racing sailboat, registered in Bermuda, insisted on the right of way of sail over steam. He had the right of way, but they had the ship.

It was almost too late when the sailboat skipper realized that the cruise ship was not going to alter course to avoid him, even though he was sailing directly across its path. He swung the boom of the sail in a last moment tacking maneuver. Instead of crossing in front of the prow of the big ship, he managed to swing the sailboat around so that both craft were traveling in the same direction. The sailboat went up and over the ship's bow wave, which leaned it in toward the ship. The tip of its tall mast scraped along the side of the ship.

On the rope ladder, Alex saw it coming and yelled a warning below him to Dante. The photographer looked and saw the mast top coming his way. He had a sudden burst of energy and climbed seven rungs in less than three seconds. The tip of the big aluminum mast passed a few inches beneath the soles of his feet.

On shore, a middle-aged tourist couple approached two fishermen repairing tackle. "Look at that big ship," the male visitor said. "Isn't it coming in way too fast this close to the harbor?"

"No English," one fisherman said. The other shrugged. Both smiled.

"He's right, you know," the fisherman said in Dutch after the couple had moved on. "It's way too fast this close to the harbor."

"That ship is not coming into the harbor," the other man scoffed. "It's too big."

"At the knots it's traveling, too late now for it to go anywhere else."

They paused in their work to take a serious look. Their experienced eyes told them a lot. They began shouting to people in Dutch, French, and English.

Elsewhere in the harbor, people were blissfully unaware of the leviathan bearing down on them. Even those who noticed the ship regarded it only as a mild diversion in a paradise where nothing ever happened.

"Look at the big white ship coming toward us," a restless child said to his mother.

She was sunbathing on a sailboat deck, her skin gleaming with oil. Raising her head and lifting her sunglasses, she took a peek. "Oh, yes, it's pretty," she said, and lay back again.

Alex helped Dante over the deck rail and they made their way to the bridge. Juliano, his arm in a sling, was on his feet. Merced and Ashton stood next to him.

"Where are the anchor controls?" Alex asked.

Juliano nodded to Merced, who hit a button marked PORT ANCHOR. The system worked. The anchor dropped with a mighty splash and the chain ran out behind it. Hitting the sandy floor of the bay, it dragged without gaining a hold. Finally, it snagged on a rock and the chain pulled taut. The force of the ship's full momentum was brought to bear on the anchor. The rock on the sea bottom held. Something had to give. One link in the chain was weaker than the others—it uncurled from its oval shape until it was nearly straight and the chain parted. The ship rushed onward.

"We're slowing down," Merced announced, hunched over the speed indicator. "Fourteen knots . . . thirteen knots . . . Come on, baby."

Ashton was looking at the sailboats ahead of them. Grabbing the ship's wheel, he yelled, "Out of the way! Please get the hell out of my way!"

Twisting the useless wheel this way and that,

Ashton tried to avoid small craft as they entered the harbor. "Where's the horn?" he asked.

Dante started pressing buttons, hoping one might be the horn.


A brunette in a skimpy swimsuit sunbathed on the hardwood deck of a very large catamaran, the *Romeo & Julia*, out of Nassau. Beside her, on the deck, were a portable TV, a CD player and stereo speakers, magazines, a telephone, and other creature comforts. A handsome guy with carefully coiffed hair came out of the cabin with two tall drinks on a silver tray. Ashton, on the bridge of the *Seabourn Legend*, was close enough to recognize them as Bloody Mary's. The guy with the drinks looked up and saw the knife edge of a tall prow headed right for him. He dropped the tray of drinks.

The brunette tilted down her shades to see what was going on. She saw—and shrieked at the top of her lungs. She went one way, and he went the other. An instant later the cruise ship's prow passed through the middle of the catamaran, splitting it in half.

When Ashton last saw them, as they disappeared out of his view on the bridge, he was desperately turning the wheel to avoid them. Now he rushed to the starboard wing of the bridge house to try to see what had become of the catamaran. "I think I just killed some rich people," he said.

• • •

The two most adventurous divers in the harbor scuba school popped their heads out of the water much farther than the herd of wimps they were learning with. They knew they'd gone way beyond where they were told to go, but it was their ass and their money, so what? Heads out of the water, they saw something that the instructors had warned them about: when a boat comes at you, go deep. This was no boat. This was a ship. They went deep, so far down they groveled in the sand at the bottom.

Not far above their bodies, a giant keel and underside passed over, like an alien spaceship in a movie. They could have reached up and touched the barnacles on it. They didn't.

But menacing as the *Seabourn Legend* appeared to those on the seabed beneath it, the ship looked even worse to the sobbing, half-naked people on its uppermost deck.

"Everybody lay flat on the deck!" Harvey urged, demonstrating the technique alongside Debbie.

"I can't believe there's still more," Ruby remarked to Fran.

"Even *I* am kind of surprised," Fran conceded.

All in all, they considered Harvey's advice to be good, and went around getting people to lie down.

• • •

Turning the ship's wheel didn't achieve a thing, but Ashton felt he at least had to try. After they tried to drop the starboard anchor and it stuck, Ashton spun the wheel hard to try to avoid two sixty-foot yachts anchored in the ship's path. The cruise ship hit the first yacht near the stern and lifted it out of the water on top of the second. The sound of this was enough to rouse the most deeply relaxed vacationers who thought they had escaped from it all.

The ship next slammed into both piggybacked yachts, catching them midship and denting them so badly with the prow, they ended up a bit U-shaped. One yacht was tossed aside like an empty cigarette box, and the other rode the prow for a few seconds before it too was cast away.

These impacts slowed the ship slightly, but this was not much help now that the cruise ship was already in the harbor, only a few hundred yards from shore and threatening to plow into scores of small craft, many with people aboard.

At this moment, Dante located the ship's steam whistle and sounded blast after blast. These warnings were very late and, if anything, only added to the confusion.

Ashton could barely bring himself to look through the bridge windows anymore. When he did, he saw people diving off sailboats and swimming for their lives. Others in tourist paddleboats paddled furiously out of the way.

About the only people along the shoreline and in the harbor who still were not aware of impending disaster were a girl in a rental speedboat and the guy she was towing behind on water skis. They were having such fun together, they weren't noticing the rest of the world. And this was the first time anyone had let her loose in a speedboat . . .

The guy on the water skis saw the big ship and waved and shouted at the girl driving the speedboat. She waved back. He thought of letting go of the towline as the ship neared them, but that would be like abandoning the girl, so he hung on. For a while it looked like the speedboat and ship would meet head on. The speedboat won by a few feet, as the girl looked up, astonished, aware for the first time that she'd been in a race. The prow cut the towline. The water skier took a spectacular spill but stayed clear of the ship. The powerful pull on the towline and its sudden release when severed changed the speedboat's course. Its driver no longer in control, the speedboat headed for shore nearby.

At the outdoor café's tables, the customers were already on their feet to get a better view, so it was only a matter of running for their lives as the speedboat came up on the sand and poked its way among the tables. Normally, that would have caused a big stir in a quiet town like this. But this morning it was hardly noticeable, except to the people who had to get out of the way fast. A few took the opportunity to sneak away without paying their bills.

Ashton saw a huge yacht right in front of them. The ship was not going to toss this yacht aside as it had the previous two, which had been merely big. This thing was humongous, at least 150 feet long, with two smokestacks, three decks, and a helipad. This was some canoe.

Turning on the ship-to-ship address system— Ashton was beginning to find his way around on the bridge—he bellowed, "Everybody wake up! There's a really big ship coming right at you!"

As Alex saw the size of the yacht, he rushed to the wheel to help Ashton spin it. Nothing happened. Instead, the *Seabourn Legend* neatly cut the yacht in half and continued undeterred. The two halves of the yacht fell over like newly cut slices of cake.

That was when a fuel boat painted bright red puttered its way across their bow.

"Oh, God!" Ashton howled. "Not again!"

The prow of the cruise ship passed within nine inches or so of the fuel boat's stern.

But the fuel boat was only a small opener for the big show still ahead. That was the island of St. Martin, which wasn't going anywhere.

"Everybody hold on fast," Alex said, staring grimly out a bridge window.

"Hit the deck!" Juliano ordered.

Merced searched for good news on the ship's speed

indicator. He had good and bad news. "We're down to ten knots," he said, "but we're gonna run aground."

Ashton couldn't think of anything to say, but he felt this was the proper time to sound nautical. He shouted, "Batten down the hatches!"

Up on the sky deck, where the passengers cowered on the floor, Liza rose and looked out a window. "There's Front Street," she said in her loud voice. "You can see the duty-free shops from here!"

On shore, a real estate agent showed a young couple and their six-year-old son a new condo. While the salesman talked, the little boy looked out a window.

"Mommy, there's a ship," he said.

"I know," she answered, with a loving smile. "There's lots of ships, honey."

"What a cute boy," the salesman said unctuously, "and very smart to notice all those ships."

The kid went on staring out the window. He watched the big ship head for the pier.

"Two bedrooms, dining room, kitchen nook—hardwood floors," the salesman was saying. "These babies will last forever."

"Mom, look!" the boy called. "It's really big."

She gave the salesman an apologetic smile and left him to talk to her husband while she went to her son. The salesman shot a dagger's look in the kid's direction.

Meanwhile on the bridge of the *Seabourn Legend*, Alex was also looking out the window. There was nothing else he could do. He watched the ship hit the pier, from which the people had fortunately run. The wood slats of the pier rose in the air, like tossing a bunch of toothpicks. One little dog wasn't putting up with this. The terrier ran out on what remained of the pier, baring its teeth and barking at the rogue ship.

Then the cruise ship's prow crashed head on into the seawall—and continued over it through a large and presumably very expensive outdoor sculpture. The impact against the seawall threw passengers forward. Most just slid on the deck and were not hurt. But in the bridge house, Alex and Juliano were thrown forward through the windows. The safety glass popped out of the frames and did not shatter or cut them—but they were left sliding forward head first on their bellies down the steep glass front of the ship, toward the prow.

As the two men slid forward and down, the ship crashed through the boardwalk, splintering it. With a rumble like hell itself opening up, the sharp keel, pushed by the ship's forward momentum, gouged a canyon through the asphalt.

"Here it comes," the little boy in the condo said to his approaching mother, not wanting her to miss the sight.

"The really great thing about Saint Martin," the salesman was saying to the boy's father, while silently cursing the racket going on outside, and whoever was causing it, "is that it's not inundated with tourists."

The mother* reached the window, glanced outside, screamed, grabbed her son and ran for their lives.

The ship sliced the condo in half, with the family and salesman all in the same half. They were left standing a few feet away from the sliding and grinding steel wall of the now slowly advancing ship. The entire building shook but remained intact. The adults were wordless in shock.

The little kid punched air and said, "Mommy, I like this place!"

The ship carried forward, nosing right into the town. One pair of late risers who were having fun in bed stopped what they were doing to stare out their window at the ship's wall cruising by, portholes no more than ten feet away.

A large speeding truck—the driver giving it the gas on his accustomed route—hung a left and ran smack into the moving curved underside of the ship. The driver stayed put behind the wheel, staring through his cracked windshield at the moving monster scraping away his radiator and front fender.

On the streets, people ran for their lives only a few feet in front of the juggernaut. A vendor shoved her pushcart loaded with tropical fruit out of the way at the very last second. Parked cars were flicked aside like miniature toys. Power lines snapped by the ship's hull sparkled and snapped like firecrackers. The terrier had scampered from the pier and was now running alongside the ship, yapping ferociously and threatening to take a bite out of its side.

A local man, with his hands full of shopping bags, came out of a store and saw the ship slicing up the street. He stopped in his tracks. A terrible thought occurred to him. His convertible, parked in front of the church, was right in the path of this ship. That was all he could think of—not why the ship was there on dry land in the first place, but what it would do to his car. Paralyzed with apprehension, he watched the sharp, steel, six-story-high prow slide through the street asphalt toward his newly polished, beloved convertible.

The terrier was now running faster than the ship, passing it and still barking like mad. The ship prow missed the convertible and slid on toward the church. The terrier stopped next to the man with the shopping bags, who was now smiling because of his car's narrow escape. The dog growled at the ship as it finally ground to a stop outside the church. The upper part of the prow gently hit the church tower and made the church bell toll.

The man put down his shopping bags and walked, stunned, toward his miraculously preserved car. The dog went with him, even more aggressive toward the ship now that it had stopped moving. Barking wildly, the terrier jumped onto the hood of the convertible to get in the ship's face. Standing next to his car, the man heard something above his head. He looked up and saw the anchor dropping.

The huge anchor came down on top of the convertible, rendering it a lump of shapeless metal. The anchor was followed by a hundred feet of heavy steel chain, which finished off anything the anchor hadn't already destroyed. The little dog vanished in the mess, its barking now silenced.

The cruise ship rested smack in the middle of the street, like a great beached whale, tilted fifteen degrees to one side and dwarfing all the buildings except the church tower. Its giant propeller still spun purposelessly in air.

The local man backed away from his ruined car and picked up his shopping bags. He wanted to leave, but couldn't. He was too distraught. Paying no attention to the big ship in the town street, he gazed at the twisted metal that had once been his car, almost invisible now beneath the anchor and piled chain links.

He heard a yapping noise then, and from beneath the chain, the terrier appeared. Totally enraged now, the little dog opened its teeth wide and went for the side of the ship.

It was a bumpy ride down the glass-topped sloping front of the ship, from the bridge to the prow. The slope stopped well before the prow, however, dropping fifteen feet down to a big Jacuzzi. Alex and Juliano came down head first on their bellies. Juliano knew for certain that these were the last moments of his life, and even Alex developed a doubt or two along the way—but neither had much chance for introspection, what with the noise and level of discomfort. They both pitched into the Jacuzzi, which fortunately for them was filled with water.

"Dammit!" Juliano croaked as soon as he got his head above water. "I think I broke my other arm."

Standing in the Jacuzzi's whirling water in his wrecked tuxedo, Alex was too busy watching the roofs of buildings passing by to pay much attention to Juliano. When the church bell rang after the prow tapped the church tower, he remembered that earlier he'd almost asked Annie to marry him. They would have a church wedding, he had no doubt about that. Also, he vaguely wondered if he might have hit his head on something. He was definitely feeling a little giddy.

High above him, on the sky deck, which now had a panoramic view of the town and whole island, the passengers wept with relief and congratulated one another on surviving this nightmare voyage whose hell had continued long into daylight. But they had lived to tell the tale. They were on dry land once more. . . .

The sky deck heaved under these passengers as the ship tilted farther sideways. They were thrown down toward the deck rail, beyond which was a drop into the street below. Clutching each other, the rail, and anything else they could find, they saved themselves from falling over the side.

The ship tilted sideways once more, coming to rest against some buildings that started sprouting cracks in their walls, solid as thin ice.

•     •     •

When he looked back and saw what had happened to the *Seabourn Legend,* Geiger whooped and hollered. He turned a loop on the sea with the Wind-Jet. This finale had not been as explosive as he might have wished, but he could live with it.

In her own way, Annie was just as pleased as he was. She figured that Alex had probably survived the ship's running aground. While Geiger celebrated, she returned with new determination to the problem of setting herself free.

Geiger surprised Annie by veering around the small island off St. Martin, instead of landing on it. She soon saw what he was up to. On the other side of the small island, a seaplane rode in the water, moored to a buoy.

"There it is," Geiger said with satisfaction.

Annie saw that if she was going to get free, it would have to be before they reached the seaplane. Geiger was so busy exulting, she was able to move her foot, unseen by him, to a lever marked RELEASE. Because her wrists were bound to the front of her jet ski, this was not an easy maneuver for her. She wasn't sure what this lever might release, but she had high hopes. Still unseen by Geiger, who was taking another look back at the cruise ship among the town buildings, she used her foot to press down hard on the lever. It didn't budge. So she got her toes underneath it before Geiger spotted what she was doing and pushed up. This time the lever gave way. . . .

The connection between the two jet skis came loose and was left behind them, floating in the sea. As the jet skis parted, Geiger's traveled onward for the seaplane, while Annie managed to use her arms to steer hers in a wide curve and head back toward the harbor.

"Annie!" Geiger yelled after her, and brought his jet ski around to give chase.

In the manner of a grand prix motorcycle road racer, she crouched down on her machine, head low, doing her best to steer with her arms. Even in a calm sea this was not easy, because the jet ski tended to bounce as it picked up speed.

Still, Annie took this opportunity to use her hands to open the lid of a storage compartment in front of the steering and rummage around to see what she could find. She discovered a flare gun and some flares. Awkwardly, because of her hands' lack of freedom to move, she pushed a flare into the gun, wondering if she'd put the correct end in.

Meanwhile, Geiger had caught up and was drawing alongside. With her wrists bound, she had to wait until they were almost elbow-to-elbow on the jet skis before, with both hands, she aimed the flare gun at his face and pulled the trigger.

Alex climbed out of the Jacuzzi and extended a hand to Juliano, who shook his head and turned his back so he could be lifted out by the armpits.

Juliano moaned with pain and staggered a bit after Alex got him standing on the deck.

Alex stood by, lending him support. "Are you all right now?" he asked finally, wanting to get going. At the same time, he admired the way the ship's officer was minimizing his injuries.

"I think I broke my other arm, and the ship's parked in the middle of town, but it could've been worse," Juliano replied, smiling through his pain. "I'm not sure how exactly, but it could've been worse."

Alex didn't bother to mention that they were in a foreign country and that TV news reporters would be on their way in another two minutes. The water sloshing out of the Jacuzzi had made the deck slippery, as Alex discovered when he tried to walk away, saying, "I have to"—then slipped and slid down the wet tilted deck—"get Annie."

He slid under the deck rail and disappeared over the side. Landing on a roof, he descended in a shower of tiles onto an ornate balcony with wrought-iron furniture and potted plants. Getting to his feet, Alex walked through an open French door into a large room containing five frightened people. He murmured something about wanting to use the stairs to their front door and went on his way.

Having just seen a cruise liner park on the street outside their house, the people in the room thought nothing of an unshaven American in the remains of a tuxedo coming in the window in order to use the stairs.

. . . . . . . . . . .

On the bridge of the *Seabourn Legend*, Ashton was still clutching the ship's wheel and looking straight ahead over the rooftops with the haunted eyes of the Ancient Mariner. Merced and Dante stood on either side of him, gazing out the empty frames where the bridge windows had been. No one mentioned Juliano or Alex, their lost shipmates, though they were on every man's mind. The three men were still sure of nothing—that this voyage was over, that they were home from the sea.

An equally confused priest stood at an ornate window in the church tower, looking out at the ship. Ashton waved to him. After a pause, the priest hesitantly waved back—like someone might wave back to invading aliens in their spaceship who showed initial signs of friendliness.

Ashton appeared to see a divine message in this. He said, "I think I'm going to church."

Harvey was enthusing at the rail of the sky deck: "People have to pay for a view like this! Come here, Debbie, take a look!"

"I ain't going near that rail, Harvey," she said. "I been through enough already. Anyway, you got no sense of shame, standing there with no pants on, so the whole town can see you in your underwear."

Harvey looked down at his bare knees and saw that she was right. He blushed and backed away from the rail, blustering, "I think people already got enough on their minds not to be bothering about me, honey."

The fact that these two were squabbling again was a sign that things were returning to normal.

Drew and her parents were signing among themselves and laughing.

"You guys are not so bad," Drew signed to them.

"Well, I'm glad someone got something positive out of this cruise," her father signed.

"At least it wasn't boring," Drew signed, and looked up to wave at Fran and Ruby, on another of their mercy missions.

"Every time we make a complete round of everyone," Fran said, "I swear something new happens."

"It makes you wonder what's going to be next," Ruby added.

"Everything's finished," Celeste said in a would-be confident voice. "Our troubles are all over now."

"I wouldn't bet the farm on that, lady," Fran said in a businesslike way, and moved on, leaving Drew and Rupert to comfort Celeste.

Farther along the deck, Sheri noticed that Liza was about to start organizing people again. "Sit down!" she said sharply.

Liza wasn't that easily discouraged. She knew she had a job to do. "I've got to think of something until we can get everyone down to the stores," she explained. "Shopping will relax their nerves." She looked closely at Sheri. "Why don't you go find an instrument and play music for us?" she asked.

All the members of Sheri's band had left on the lifeboats. Sheri wished she'd gone with them. The kind of thing that had happened to them on this ship might be interesting on a newscast happening to someone else, she supposed, but it did nothing for her career. She looked at Liza with a sarcastic smile and took a mouth organ from her pocket.

Liza's face lit up. Her voice boomed, "Ladies and gentlemen—"

Sheri caught her by the throat and held the mouth organ as if she intended to stuff it down.

Liza asked, "Why are you so hostile to me?"

Just a few feet away, Frank was worrying about his wife. "Constance," he said, "is there anything you need?"

She looked at him impatiently. "Why, Frank, do you have a selection of goods to offer?"

"No, actually . . ." His voice trailed away.

Constance looked at him with genuine concern. "What is it?" she asked.

"You know that I never, ever smoked in my life," he said. "Well, a terrible thing has happened to me now that you've stopped."

"No!" she said.

Frank nodded. "I need a cigarette."

• • •

In shades and bright shorts, wearing a small gold record on a chain around his neck, the well-known music producer Maurice Gooding sat in his cigarette boat *Tuneman*, loading spear guns and enjoying the spectacle of the ship plowing into the town.

"Now that is some ugly driving," he said to a lithe island girl named Marifa.

"Vengeance o' moko," Marifa said.

"Say what?"

"Bad luck to run ship over town," she said.

"No shit, bad luck," Maurice agreed. "I just bought a time-share here."

Not far from them, and getting closer every moment, Alex was searching for a boat to take him to find Annie.

"I need a boat!" he told one man standing in a speedboat. "This is an emergency!"

The man pointed down, and Alex noticed that the man was up to his knees in water. It would take at least twenty minutes to pump that much water out of the boat, after which the engine might or might not start.

Alex knew he had to try elsewhere. He needed a decent boat—something fast enough to outrun a Wind-Jet. That meant something a lot sportier than the average motorboat. A lot of craft in the harbor were damaged or had taken on water. While scanning the nearby boats, his eye caught a cigarette boat moored on the seaward side of what remained of the pier. Protected by the pier, the boat looked unscathed. Alex headed for it in a hurry.

"Come on, baby, unhook that line," Maurice told Marifa. "We got some rum to drink, some fish to spear." He started the powerful engine.

Alex took a flying leap off the pier and landed on top of the cigarette boat's extended forward part as it pulled away. He quickly jumped down between the two seats and stood behind them.

Maurice almost fell out of his seat. "Can I help you?" he asked with menacing politeness.

"I'm a cop and I need to use this boat," Alex said in a law-enforcement monotone.

"This is a joke, right?" Maurice said. "You're messing with my head? Can't you see I'm on a date?"

"My name is Alex Shaw, I'm with the LAPD, and this is a matter of life and death. Now move the goddamn boat."

"LAPD? Do you know how many hours of therapy I've had because of you guys? And that shit's expensive. I think you better get off my tub."

Alex picked up a spear gun. "Just go," he said quietly.

Marifa had been watching without saying anything. "I think we go now," she said.

Maurice grudgingly settled behind the wheel. "Okay," he said, "I'll go, but you promise me you're not gonna trash my baby."

Alex set aside the spear gun and picked him out of the seat by the back of his shorts. Sitting in his place, Alex opened the throttle. The cigarette boat thrust forward, practically lifting Maurice out of the craft and into the water.

Maurice fell on his ass on the deck behind the seats and whimpered, "Just go easy, man. This puppy cost me a hundred and fifty grand."

Alex opened the engine up full and the cigarette boat's nose rose out of the water. Maurice slid backward along the deck.

Marifa relaxed in her seat and let the wind blow through her hair.

Annie's jet ski bumped on the water as she pulled the flare gun trigger. Her flare passed a few inches over Geiger's head as he traveled alongside. She saw it dawning on his face what she'd tried to do to him, and the sudden twisting of his features into rage. She could feel his eyes upon her skin.

Knowing she had to escape now, no matter what, she cut across in front of his jet ski and almost succeeded in toppling him. But he spun his jet ski around in a tight circle and came after her again. All she'd gained was a few yards on him. Hunching down on her machine, Annie tried to make every inch of those few yards count for something as she headed back toward the harbor.

But Geiger began gaining on her again, being better able to handle his jet ski, since his wrists were not bound to the front of the machine, like hers. As he came up on one side of her, he saw her fiddling with the flare gun, loading a flare into its barrel. He knew she'd love to put that flare between his eyes, but he could see that her bound wrists would not permit her to get off a shot at him until he drew level with her.

So Geiger kept behind until he'd built up enough momentum to creep close alongside her. Alert for any sudden turn she might attempt, he succeeded in getting shoulder-to-shoulder with Annie before she realized it. When she tried to aim the flare gun at Geiger, he reached out with one hand and seized the barrel, twisting it upward. The flare gun discharged and the flare rocketed into an arc high above them, exploded, and descended in picturesque white smoke plumes against the blue sky.

Having tossed the flare gun in the sea, Geiger jumped from his jet ski onto the back of Annie's. Sitting behind her, he reached around to steer her into a 180-degree curve, heading them back once more toward the seaplane.

Annie started jumping around on the jet ski then, hoping to catch him by surprise and knock him off.

"What are you trying to do?" he yelled.

"Let go of me!" she screamed, and kicked her heel back against his shin.

. . . . . . . . . . . . . . . . . . . . . . . . . .

The speedometer read seventy-five as Alex whipped the cigarette boat through a cluster of tiny unin-habited islands, hoping that Geiger had tried to hide with Annie among them.

Maurice tried a soothing conversational tone with the madman at the controls of his boat. "Did I tell you I was dropped by Allstate because of the LAPD? They said I was high risk—"

"Look!" Marifa interrupted. "Fireworks!"

Alex looked in the direction she pointed and saw the flare. He twisted the wheel and headed the cig-arette boat toward it.

"There's, uh, lots of shallow reefs around here, man," Maurice warned. "You really don't want to go too fast."

The front of the cigarette boat rose high out of the water as Alex pushed it as hard as it would go. Occasionally, things scraped off the boat's bottom, maybe reef tops or shark backs, Alex didn't slow down to check.

In spite of Annie's exertions, Geiger brought their jet ski to the seaplane. With a knife, he cut the rope from the front of the jet ski, releasing her from the machine but leaving her wrists tied together. Then he stroked her throat with the blade.

"Just climb into the plane," he ordered. "No tricks."

Holding her bound hands in front of her, Annie stepped off the jet ski onto one of the plane's pontoons. She reached up with both hands and opened the cockpit door, in front of the wing. A series of metal steps sunk in the fuselage led up into the cockpit. She looked back. Geiger was still on the jet ski, watching her carefully. He had replaced the knife with his Glock nine-millimeter pistol. She could see by the look in his eyes that it wouldn't take much at this point to goad him into squeezing the trigger. Turning around, she climbed the steps into the plane's cockpit.

After releasing the plane from its mooring line, Geiger followed her quickly, not giving her a chance to fool with the plane's controls. He toted his bag with him, which was now sheathed in a waterproof covering and had flotation devices attached. Accidentally dropping this bag in the water was an eventuality he had clearly given some thought to.

At gunpoint, she settled into the co-pilot's seat. Geiger sat beside her, in the pilot's seat. Looking over the pistol muzzle at her, he said, "Annie, I think I'm going to let you go"—he paused—"at about ten thousand feet."

When he got over laughing at his own joke, he flicked on switches and made instrument adjustments. "Give me a second," he said mockingly. "I haven't flown for years."

"Why don't you put it on autopilot?" Annie asked.

Geiger smiled to himself but refused to be drawn into reacting. Concentrating now, he kept her covered by casually laying the pistol on his lap with one hand on it. With the other, he completed flight preparations. He switched on the engine and the propeller whirred. Annie could feel the plane straining to move forward now, like a horse impatient to go.

The plane taxied some distance into the wind, picking up speed as it headed for the open sea. Confident that he was home free now, Geiger opened the throttle some more.

The seaplane skipped along the surface, almost airborne, when a cigarette boat suddenly came into sight and charged head on at the plane along its takeoff path. Both Geiger and Annie immediately recognized Alex at the boat's wheel. Geiger slowed the plane and then changed course, so it was taking off in a direction at a right angle to the previous one. He opened the throttle and the plane built up speed again. The cigarette boat would have to chase them now.

"I will say this, Annie," Geiger purred, knowing that the boat had come too late to stop the plane. "Alex is very entertaining, just like you."

Behind the plane, Alex urged on the boat, "Come on, come on!"

The cigarette boat was much faster than Geiger

had reckoned and was soon only a few yards behind the plane.

"Take over the wheel!" Alex shouted to Maurice. "Follow the plane as close as you can!"

"Give me one good reason," Maurice said sulkily from where he lay on the deck behind the seats.

"If you don't take the wheel, I'll throw you over the side!"

"That's a good reason," Marifa acknowledged.

In a hurry, Maurice took the wheel, sliding into the driver's seat. The boat drew up alongside the plane behind one wing, both doing about eighty-five miles per hour.

Aiming a spear gun at the plane, Alex shouted, "You have to get closer!"

"He's going to shoot a plane. . . ." Maurice said to anyone who was listening, rolling his eyes.

Alex shot a spear into the plane's wing. He tied off the light braided steel line to a gunwale cleat as the line tautened between the plane and boat. The spear's barbs held fast in the wing covering.

Maurice forgot his quarrel with Alex. This was the kind of stuff he enjoyed, almost like a real-life video game. He eased on the throttle a little, and the boat's slowing pulled the plane by its wing to one side. It was like a small boy tormenting a butterfly, except that Maurice as a child had never played with insects.

Marifa was happy to see the boys happy. She handed Alex another loaded spear gun.

. . .

Each time the plane was jerked sideways by one wing, Geiger had to struggle with the controls to prevent it from capsizing. The fourth time it happened, Annie saw her chance and took it. With both hands, she reached for a thermos flask beside her and hit Geiger on the head with it.

"You little shit!" Geiger moaned, dazed but still able to lean back on the yoke and try to take off.

Annie grabbed the bag of jewels and threw it out her side window. As she did so, she was shocked to see Alex right behind them!

Maurice skillfully pulled the plane back down on the water, so it was skimming over the surface again. Alex released the second spear. This one hit a pontoon. Before Alex could tie off the line to a cleat, the line pulled tight and lifted him out of the boat.

Holding on to the spear gun, he was dragged behind the plane for some yards before struggling to his feet, getting his sneakers together and water-skiing at the end of the line.

In the plane cockpit, Annie threw herself against Geiger. He hit her in one eye with his fist, knocking her back into the co-pilot's seat again.

"You're not gonna screw this up!" he snarled at her, and then tried to lift the plane off the water again.

Once more Maurice played the seaplane like a

big fish, reeled it in and set it back on the water surface. But Alex was getting badly slammed in his
high-speed waterskiing without a board. He knew
he could not hang in much longer. With nothing
else to try, he pressed the retraction button on the
spear gun. Immediately he was pulled straight
toward the pontoon in which the spear was embed-
ded. As the last few feet of line wound in, he
stepped onto the pontoon.

His weight tipped the seaplane's balance sufficiently to alert Geiger of his whereabouts. Geiger
pulled the plane hard left, hoping in one move both
to dislodge Alex and shake off the line attached to
the boat. Alex lost his grip and slipped, but hung
on to the pontoon. The line from the wing to the
boat held, the plane almost capsizing. Geiger had
to struggle once more to keep its nose out of the
water. While he was doing this, Annie elbowed him
as hard as she could on the forehead. Geiger
slumped forward onto the controls.

Alex attempted to make his way forward along
the pontoon, but the pilotless plane was now buck-
ing and behaving erratically. He edged forward of
the wing and tried to reach up to the handle of the
cockpit door on Annie's side of the plane. But he
couldn't reach it while the plane was bouncing on
the water, out of control.

Annie pulled Geiger away from the instruments
and tried to steady the plane with the yoke. Though
she had no idea what she was doing, it seemed to

make the plane run more smoothly. Now that she was concentrating on controlling the plane, she didn't notice Geiger recover consciousness.

While trying to push himself upright, Geiger saw Alex's face looking in the side window next to the co-pilot's seat. A moment later the L.A. cop opened the door and was climbing in.

Geiger leaned across and pulled back sharply on the yoke, sending the plane into a steep ascent off the water. The force was enough to tear the spear from the wing, along with a big patch of wing cover. But the plane was no longer on the boat's apron string.

The liftoff threw Annie off balance. Geiger shouldered her into Alex and then heaved them both through the cockpit doorway. They tumbled out and landed on the pontoon beneath. The impact of their weight snapped the pontoon from the plane, and they fell together astride the pontoon. Alex held on to Annie as the pontoon splashed into the sea and kept traveling like a runaway sled.

Happy to feel the seaplane rising now, free of restraint, Geiger looked ahead, expecting to find a cloudless blue sky. Instead, he saw the vast side of the supertanker *Stena Convoy*.

Still dazed from the blows to his head, Geiger lifted the
seaplane straight up the side of the supertanker, bank-
ing the plane as he barely made it over the top.
Leveling the wings over the tanker's deck, he headed
for the open skies. He was beginning to smile again,
knowing for sure now that he was home free, when he
heard a tremendous crack and the plane stalled, frozen
in midair. Not believing that this was physically possible, and thinking it might have something to do with
being hit on the head, he waited for the moment to
pass. It didn't. He was still sitting in a plane that had
become paralyzed in midair.

Looking out the side window of the cockpit, he saw
the tanker's deck beneath him. Directly underneath,

he saw the base of the ship's mast. Then the truth hit him. The sound he'd heard was the top of the steel mast piercing the belly of his plane. The seaplane was now impaled on the tanker's mast.

Pushing the plane door open, Geiger saw Annie and Alex on the pontoon. The sweethearts are back together again, he thought bitterly. But he no longer cared. He had his diamonds. Still, he would have liked to have the girl. If she'd had any sense, she would have chosen him over that stupid cop, who should have been dead by now anyway. But he was well rid of them both, he told himself. They'd made his life hell. Had it not been for them, this would have been a real pleasure cruise. . . .

For some reason, they both jumped off the pontoon. Then the girl sank! Of course, her wrists were probably still tied. He stopped a moment to watch in anticipation as Alex dived after her, being the hero as usual. Geiger scanned the water hopefully for signs of sharks.

The tanker captain got on the address system and ordered the crew to abandon ship. He told them he would stay. They must go. Immediately!

Regularly trained to evacuate the ship at speed, each member of the crew had a place to fill and a role to play in readying the two lifeboats. From the bridge, the captain watched them pile into the two modern lifeboats and pull their sliding plastic tops closed.

These lifeboats looked more like spacecraft than tra-
ditional boats, but they were unsinkable in any seas.
He watched as each craft was propelled from its chute
into the sea and took off at speed to put a safe distance between it and the ship. There was no need to
explain things to these men. When he said go, they
were gone. He hadn't been able to let them go during
the previous emergency, because they were needed to
start the engines and draw up the anchors. This time,
they could do nothing. They at least could be saved.

He had seen everything. After having taken his
ship without incident through some of the most dangerous waters in the world—through the Persian
Gulf, around Cape Horn—he'd become a victim in
these placid, blue, vacation-poster seas. With no
explanation, a cruise ship had tried to ram him,
pulling away only at the last moment and sideswip-
ing him instead. Now a small seaplane had done its
version of the same thing. What was he missing?
What did he not know about? He had never taken
this Bermuda Triangle thing seriously. Was there
something here that affected people's minds?

Well, he'd been a good captain. He had no wife,
no children. But he had saved his men's lives and he
was staying with his ship.

Geiger turned off the plane's engine. Untying the
bag of diamonds from around his waist, he checked
to make sure it was securely closed and then slung

it out the plane door. Watching its downward descent, he was relieved to see it clear the deck where the ship narrowed toward its prow. The bag splashed into the sea and floated. If he followed the same trajectory, rolled up as tightly as he could, he would survive. He kicked off his shoes, preparing for the long swim ahead. It had hurt him to part with the diamonds like this, but it would have hurt him a hell of a lot physically to hit the water with them attached to him. Putting his feet together at the edge of the doorway, he got ready to jump.

Only then did he notice the fuel gushing from his plane, spraying downward around the mast. The mast wiring had been torn loose, and two wires were sending out sparks like fireflies. Geiger stared helplessly.

He'd been so sure. Everything in his plan had been worked out, down to the finest detail. How could it have all come to this?

A cop and his girlfriend. They had done this to him.

The fuel ignited and the plane exploded. A second later the entire supertanker blew into a giant fireball that rose high over the ocean.


Alex followed Annie's stream of air bubbles down through filtered shafts of light. Then he saw her through the clear seawater, not very far beneath him. With her wrists bound, she couldn't swim. He'd known that when he pushed her off the pontoon, realizing they were getting too near the tanker for safety now that the plane was stuck on its mast. But he had not thought that Annie would sink so fast or go so far down.

Alex saw her now, sinking and struggling frantically against her bonds. Kicking strong, he swam downward and seized what was left of her black dress. Then he encircled her with one arm and made for the surface. They broke through and breathed air into their lungs. That was when they felt the heat. It was so strong they had to take a breath and go beneath the surface again.

The last thing they'd seen was an immense ship. Now there was only a sea of raging fire. Ducking frequently beneath the surface, Alex swam and Annie floated away from the conflagration. Once they got some distance and the flames died down a bit, he untied her wrists. This took some time, since he had no knife and the rope swollen with water was difficult to unknot. She massaged her wrists and anxiously looked for rope burns on her skin. They didn't say anything to each other. It was enough to look in each other's eyes and smile—and tread water.

"Slow down," Marifa ordered. "Even in calm water like this, it can be hard to see somebody. Get in a little bit closer."

Maurice grimaced but did what he was told. He

knew Marifa was right. They had to look for sur-
vivors. Anyway, the harbor authorities or police
would probably question him. This way he could
truthfully say he had tried to help, that he'd searched
and so forth. Though he didn't want any dead or
dying people messing up his boat, he didn't mind
wet people. But no blood. He continued circling the
burning remains of the tanker.

"Look!" Marifa pointed to something bobbing in
the water. "Someone's head."

It was only a black bag covered with waterproof-
ing and with some flotation devices attached.
Marifa was disappointed, but Maurice figured that
whatever was inside must be worth something if its
owner took the trouble to make sure it floated. He
reached out and hauled it aboard. He threw it in the
bottom of the boat, intending to open it later, when
he wouldn't have to share its contents.

The cigarette boat had made almost a complete
circle when Marifa called out, "There's the guy who
speared the plane. He's in the water." She added in
a disappointed tone, "He has a girl with him."

They helped Annie and Alex into the boat.

Alex untied Annie's hands and then gazed fondly
at her. She looked back at him, feeling safe once
more to be with him. But her new feeling of security
with him also released a more intense consciousness
of the terror she had been through. His reassuring
smile almost made her cry.

"You're okay?" he asked.

"I didn't think I was going to make it."

"Annie, I've got something for you."

"What?"

From his pocket he pulled the dripping wet jewelry pouch. He opened it. "Want to wear this for a while?"

Annie looked in and saw the ring. She was shocked. "How long are you thinking about?"

Alex smiled. "Fifty years."

She stared at the ring, overwhelmed. Looking into his eyes and smiling, she said, "But for the rest of our lives, I'm planning the vacations, okay?"

They kissed.

While they were embracing, Maurice reached over the side of the boat and pulled a floating bag from the water. He opened it, and the stolen convention diamonds blazed under the Caribbean sun.

"Look what I just found in international waters!" Maurice exulted. "Man, this *is* paradise! Ha ha!"

But Annie and Alex were too busy in each other's arms to pay him any attention.

Formerly an editor at various publishing houses and magazines, **GEORGE RYAN** has been writing full time for over ten years. He is the author of many action/adventure and western novels published under pseudonyms by Warner and Berkley, and also the co-author of several nonfiction books. George Ryan lives in New York City.